QUEEN OF DRAGONS

KINGDOM OF FAIRYTALES BOOK 1

J A ARMITAGE

Edited By Rose Lipscomb

Cover by Enchanted Quill Press

Proof Reader: Tina Merritt

Created with Vellum

KINGDOM OF FAIRYTALES

You all know the fairytales, the stories that always have the happy ending. But what happens after all those storybook characters get what they wanted? Is it really a happily ever after?

In this prequel, you will find out what happens next, be transported back to those lands you fell in love with and be prepared to meet some new characters along the way.

Kingdom of Fairytales is a new way of reading with one chapter a day and one book a week throughout the year beginning January 1st

Lighting-fast reads you won't be able to put down

Read in real time as each chapter follows a day in the life of a character throughout the entire year, with each bite-sized episode representing a week in the life of our hero.

Each character's story wrapped up at the end of every season with a brand new character and story featured in each season.

Fantasy has never been so epic!

READING ORDER

Kingdom of Fairytales is a 52 book series split into thirteen seasons. Each season has a four book story arc of a fairytale character with the last season seeing them all coming together. You can read any series first with the exception of thirteen, however it is recommended that you read in the order below…

PREQUEL

SLEEPING BEAUTY

1. Queen of Dragons
2. Heiress of Embers
3. Throne of Fury
4. Goddess of Flames

LITTLE MERMAID

5. Queen of Mermaids
6. Heiress of the Sea
7. Throne of Change
8. Goddess of Water

RED RIDING HOOD

9. King of Wolves
10. Heir of the Curse
11. Throne of Night
12. God of Shifters

RAPUNZEL

13. King of Devotion
14. Heir of Thorns
15. Throne of Enchantment
16. God of Loyalty

RUMPELSTILTSKIN

17. Queen of Unicorns
18. Heiress of Gold
19. Throne of Sacrifice
20. Goddess of Loss

BEAUTY AND THE BEAST

21. King of Beasts
22. Heir of Beauty
23. Throne of Betrayal
24. God of Illusion

ALADDIN

25. Queen of the Sun
26. Heiress of Shadows
27. Throne of the Phoenix
28. Goddess of Fire

CINDERELLA

29. Queen of Song
30. Heiress of Melody
31. Throne of Symphony

32. Goddess of Harmony

ALICE IN WONDERLAND

33. Queen of Clockwork
34. Heiress of Delusion
35. Throne of Cards
36. Goddess of Hearts

WIZARD OF OZ

37. King of Traitors
38. Heir of Fugitives
39. Throne of Emeralds
40. God of Storms

SNOW WHITE

41. Queen of Reflections
42. Heiress of Mirrors
43. Throne of Wands
44. Goddess of Magic

PETER PAN

45. Queen of Skies
46. Heiress of Stars
47. Throne of Feathers
48. Goddess of Air

URBIS

49. Kingdom of Royalty
50. Kingdom of Power
51. Kingdom of Fairytales
52. Kingdom of Ever After

URBIS PRISON
SHIPLEY
THE VALE
AZREN
BADALAH
DESERT
KISBU
DRACONIS
ZHORE
MOSA
ELDER
ABORIA
AZURE
ENCHANTIA
URBIS
SKYLA
EMERALD CITY
OZ
FLORIS
TULIS
THE FORGE
ARCADIA
RENAIS
MELFALL
ATLANTICE
ANTLA
W
E
S
KINGDOM
OF
FAIRYTALES

PROLOGUE

No one understands what it's like when your mother is famous for her beauty, and you are, at best, average. Actually, I'm wrong. She wasn't famous just for her beauty, but that's how people tell the story, how people have always told the story. That was even her name for a while. No one remembered her real name. She was just the sleeping princess or Sleeping Beauty. Even all these years later, when the royals appear in the paper, my father, the king, barely gets a mention, and I'm only a footnote in my own life, destined to always be Sleeping Beauty's daughter

My name's Princess Azia Rose of Draconis, and here is my story...

1ST JANUARY

The sword glinted in the sun, golden flecks of light, turning to orange as the sun began its trek to the other side of the world. His colossal height dwarfed me, giving him the advantage in every way. He stood at nearly six feet five, towering over me, and his strength was unsurpassed in all the kingdom. I dodged him as he ruthlessly attacked, thrusting his sword at me mercilessly and without care. The complexities of sword fighting did not interest him. His aim was only to kill, his one desire to see his blade thrust deep into my belly. I danced around him as time after time he attacked, and I put into practice all the defense strategies I'd learned from watching my younger brothers' training. Training that, as a girl, I'd never received, and yet, here I was, embroiled in a fight to the death with a giant of a man. I knew how to handle a sword. Even without official training, I rivaled most men in the art of combat, but as my attacker wasn't schooled in good sportsmanship and his technique involved him waving his sword around haphazardly, there was very little I could do to anticipate where his next attack would come from. I thought that I'd be able to see it in his eyes, the little tells that would give away where he would next thrust his sword, but he was focused on the kill, and there was no telling where the sword would go next.

He murmured as he fought, a strange language known only to himself. A pep talk? Who knew?

I swerved to the side as he rushed at me full force, his blade missing me by inches. A momentary thrill of celebration ran through me, but it was short-lived. I'd barely turned back toward him when the full length of his sword was thrust into my side, right up to the hilt.

Tumbling to the ground, I clutched my belly, wailing in agony and then became still. My eyes closed, and my screams were silenced. I was dead.

Beside me, he giggled and rubbed his hands in gleeful euphoria. His enormous size made the ground beneath me shake with his quivering body as he too fell to the ground beside me.

With one of my eyes open, just a slit, I watched as my brother, Remy wailed in rapturous joy. I suppressed a grin. The dead don't smile, but it was difficult not to when his laughter was so infectious. He must have looked strange to an outsider, giggling like a young child, because that's essentially what he was. With the body of a man and the mind of a toddler, outsiders rarely understood him. Picking his trick sword up, I handed it back to him with a smile. He stabbed me a few more times in the belly for good measure, the fake blade retracting up into the hilt every time, and with every thrust, another giggle erupted from his mouth.

"Okay now," I said, ruffling his overly shaggy dark brown hair. "Time for dinner."

"Ta Aza." He pulled himself up into a standing position, the grin of victory still plastered on his gorgeous face. He pulled me into a bear hug, which was much more dangerous than the sword fight as he didn't know his own strength. As a young child, he'd broken my arm similarly, and since then, I'd had to use a safe word with him to make him let go for fear of being crushed to death in his muscular arms.

"Unsquash," I gasped, and he let go of me immediately.

"Uhsqua Aza," he repeated back to me in the best way he knew how. He pronounced my name as Aza although it was Azia. I loved hearing it because, of all my other siblings, mine was the only one he even attempted.

I felt rather than saw someone's eyes on us. Turning my attention away from Remy, I scanned the surrounding field. In the distance, the royal castle rose majestically against a backdrop of the Fire Mountains. The base of the mountain range was covered with thick purple heather, which gave the grey stone of the castle a pinkish hue in the evening light. As they rose into the clouds, they assumed a deep brilliant hue of red - one of the reasons the Fire Mountains got their name, the other being the dragons that lived up in the peaks.

The stone bridge leading from the main entrance away from the open portcullis was quiet as was usual this time of day, and the surrounding fields showed no sign of life except the castle horses sharing the field with us and the occasional fire butterfly that fluttered around our heads. Glancing back at Remy, I saw that he was engrossed in a flower—one of his many obsessions.

I couldn't see anyone else in the field with us, but the hairs on the back of my neck prickled, and the quietness set my teeth on edge. Scanning the perimeter of the field again, I finally saw him. Tall and blond, he stood against one of the Manzanita trees that dotted around the field. That's why I'd not seen him before. The reddish-brown of his clothes blended with the bark he leaned against. His hair was long and, at closer inspection, was not blond at all, but almost silver. The wind toyed with it, sweeping the ass-length locks out behind him in a wave of free hair and braids. He was too far away for me to see his features properly, but I didn't need to see the points of his ears to know he was a faery. I felt his magical energy even from here.

My stomach churned at the sight of him, and I shivered as his cold energy passed through my body.

"Come on, Remy, It's time to go to dinner." I stood and held my hand out for my brother to take.

"No, Aza." He pointed to the flower. He didn't want to pick it. He only wanted to sit with it, looking at it and occasionally stroking the delicate petals. That's why our castle garden was full of weeds and dandelions; he refused to let the gardeners pull the weeds up, not that much grew around here anyway in the deep-red Draconis soil.

"We can come back and look at the flower tomorrow," I urged restlessly. The faery watched us, making me nervous. Fae were not natural in Draconis, so he had to be from one of the other kingdoms where magic was more prolific. Enchantia, maybe, where they all knew magic. That made him a stranger, and I didn't like strangers. Especially ones that were unbidden. "It needs to sleep," I added. Sometimes I had to be a little economical with the truth when it came to Remy; otherwise, I'd have to drag him, and as he was twice my size, that just wasn't happening.

I took his hand, leading him back to the castle, brushing the dirt from my leather clothing as I went. I was a princess, and I didn't do dirt. At least, I wasn't supposed to.

We crossed the field to the gate, which would lead us to the castle bridge. It meant we would pass the faery. He kept his eyes fixed on me as we got closer, putting me more on edge. His windswept hair was only the crowning glory to the beauty that sat below it. Tight muscular arms told me he was a fighter; some kind of warrior from another kingdom. My nerves clenched as we walked the path toward him. He held a sword in one hand—a work of art with amethyst stones in the hilt, and the other arm was casually draped on the tree next to him. As I got closer, I saw his eyes were the same color as the stones in his sword, giving an impression of otherworldliness. A pale purple that was no less dazzling for their lightness in color. I sucked in a breath at how beautiful he was. Utter perfection in faery form. No one in Draconis looked the way he did, and yet, the expression on his face was one of disgust. He wrinkled his nose and sneered at us as we got close to him.

I'd hoped to ignore him as we passed by, but he opened his mouth to speak. I readied myself with a hello on my lips. As a princess, my parents schooled me to be courteous to the people, even the awful ones, but it seemed he didn't have the same schooling as I.

"Is he some kind of idiot?" He nodded to Remy, who gave him a smile. Remy didn't understand what this man was saying, and even if he did, he would have loved him anyway. Remy loved everyone. Unfortunately, I understood perfectly, and his words sickened me to my stomach.

Clenching my teeth, I remembered what my mother had told me about politeness. Then I promptly forgot it. "With a remark like that, there's only one idiot around here, and Prince Remy isn't it."

I shot him a look that was certainly not fit for a princess and stalked past him, Remy's hand in mine, my breath held. I'd never insulted anyone before, but then again, I'd never heard anyone dare insult Remy in my presence before. The faery was lucky I didn't have my real sword on me, and that killing him would probably annoy my mother, not to mention getting blood on my tunic.

The energy the faery possessed coursed through my body as I walked by him, but I refused to look his way again, even though I could barely breathe with the force of it. Picking up my pace, I practically ran Remy over the bridge, and once through to the castle courtyard, I ordered the guards to close the portcullis. It was a little early—usually, it closed at sundown and reopened at dawn; but, although surprised by my command, the guards did as I asked. Being the heir to the throne did have its perks sometimes.

I was still fuming about the stranger when Remy and I traipsed into the castle dining hall. It was one of two. The grand hall we used for formal occasions and this one—the family dining room, which was just for us and our special guests should we have them. This evening, it was just the five of us. Mother, Remy, my younger brothers, Ash and Hollis, and lastly, me. My father often skipped dinners due to work commitments, and as he wasn't at the table, he would probably be at his desk in his study.

"Azia," My mother admonished, twirling her eyes skyward as she always did when I came indoors covered in mud. "Couldn't you, at least, wash up before coming to dinner? You are a princess, not a swineherd."

As if I was ever allowed to forget. She mentioned it at least five times a day!

"Sorry Ma," I said, kissing her cheek and sitting in my place at the giant oval dinner table. The second I sat down, one of the castle servants brought a bowl of soup, placing it on the table in front of me.

"Ooee Ma," Remy parroted, kissing her cheek and following my lead.

My mother's mouth quirked to the side as her eldest son kissed her, and all at once, I knew she would be mad no longer. Remy was my secret weapon. It didn't matter how awful a daughter I was or how unkempt I came in for dinner. Remy would always back me up.

My mother's face beamed and the beauty she was famous for shone out. Her gorgeous golden hair settled in waves down her back before curling under the bottom edges, and her makeup-free skin was flawless. She was the famous Sleeping Beauty, after all.

"You'll have to get ready for tonight after dinner," she said, turning her gaze back to me, now that Remy was happily tucking into his dinner. "I can't have my only daughter looking like an urchin. I've left a dress out on your bed and instructed your maid to turn that's rat's tail you call hair into something fit for a princess."

All around me, the scrape of forks against plates sounded out as my three brothers ate like we had no more food coming, despite eating a fine dinner every night. If anyone looked like street urchins, it was them, but that was ok because they were boys and boys were allowed to do what they pleased and look how they pleased. It was only I, as the daughter of the famous Sleeping Beauty that had expectations to live up to. Even though my father was the highest in all the land, his fame was eclipsed by the woman he married. And because of my mother's fame throughout all the kingdoms as the most beautiful woman to have ever lived, people expected me to be the same...except I wasn't. I wasn't even close, a fact that the press liked to point out at any given opportunity much to my chagrin.

Like her, I was blonde, but dark blonde that almost bordered on brown. My hair didn't have the same gold that ran through my mother's hair, catching the light, giving her the look of an angel. It was also, as my mother was keen to point out, usually a mess. Not that I could be completely blamed for it. Her hair had beautiful waves. Mine had unruly curls. Add that to the fact that I was adopted. There was no way in Draconis. I could look like my mother, and yet, everyone seemed to expect it. Expect it and then point out how disappointed they were that I didn't.

I sighed and caught my reflection in the back of a spoon. I

still had mud on my nose. "What's happening tonight?" I asked casually, putting the spoon down and splashing tomato soup all over the clean white tablecloth while trying to remember what particular royal occasion I'd forgotten now.

"Your father wants you to meet someone, that's all," she replied airily, as though she'd not just dropped a bomb on me. Her words even caused two of my three brothers stopping eating and looking up from their plates.

"Who wants to meet Azia?" Ash, my middle brother asked, soup dripping down his chin, reminding me of a vampire after a kill. He ran his fingers through his long brown hair to pull it back from his face. At sixteen, he was turning into quite the looker. In fact, all of my brothers shared some of the beauty of my mother. All of them had her long eyelashes and high cheekbones, but they all got their square chins, dark brown hair, and height from my father. As the only adopted member of the family, I was always painfully aware that I stood out amongst them.

"Never you mind. That's between Azia and your father," she said, sipping tea from the daintiest little cup, her little finger raised in perfect etiquette. Rosebud lips sipped at the tea, and I knew for a fact, that she wouldn't leave a lipstick stain on the teacup. Those cherry lips were all her.

Ash and Hollis' eyes swiveled towards me, and I knew what they wanted. They wanted me to ask who I was going to be meeting. Normally, I would let them suffer and carry on eating as though I didn't care, but curiosity burned through me. No one ever asked to speak to just me. I was only one member of the royal family and not a particularly interesting one to boot.

"Who is it, mother?"

She placed her teacup back on the saucer and gave me a

warm smile, her eyes crinkling up at the edges. "You shall see after you've gotten yourself cleaned up. Now, eat your dinner before it gets cold."

A picture of the man I'd seen earlier flittered through my mind. I could still feel the energy he possessed even though he was no longer near. He had nothing to do with whatever it was my father wanted me for, but the coincidence of there being a stranger near the castle didn't sit well in my stomach, and after finishing my soup, I couldn't eat any more.

"Where are you going?" Mother asked as I took my leave from the table.

I took the napkin from around my neck and threw it on the table. "I'm not hungry. I'm going to do as you asked and get ready for Father." The quicker I found out what was going on, the sooner I could relax.

This brought a smile to her face. I left the room, my stomach in knots. Yes, I was the heir to the throne of Draconis, but up until now, my main responsibility had been to wear pretty dresses and be an accessory to my mother's beauty like a designer bag from Urbis or The Forge.

My maid Dahlia took one look at me and ordered me into the bath right away. She was a plump woman of about forty with permanently ruddy cheeks and a friendly smile. Not that her smile fooled me. She'd been my maid and governess since I was born, and I knew, behind that mild exterior, she was smart as a whip and took no-nonsense. As she worked on lathering up my hair, chattering away about her son who was failing in school, my mind drifted back to the stranger I'd seen earlier, making my stomach churn even more.

Once my bath was over, Dahlia worked on my hair, brushing the knots out and doing the best she could with my unruly curls. Next, she moved onto my face, expertly applying makeup. She really was an all-rounder, and that's why she'd spent so many years looking after me. She could turn her hand to anything. She was the only person in the whole kingdom my mother trusted to do my makeup for me. She certainly didn't trust me with it. Apparently the "just drawn on by a four-year-old with a crayon" look was not what my mother wanted, so Dahlia did it all. I happily let her.

Taking a deep breath, I tried to rid myself of the energy buzzing around my body. My heart was beating much quicker than normal, and the bath had failed to put me at ease. No matter what I did, the image of the man with the long silver hair kept coming back to me. The way he'd looked at me with such disdain. It hadn't been directed at Remy, despite the fact it was Remy he'd mentioned. He'd been looking at me; his piercing pale purple eyes had drawn me in. Now that I'd had time to think about it, I wondered if he'd used some kind of magic on me. It would explain the pounding in my chest and the electricity buzzing through my veins.

"There! All finished. You look beautiful."

I opened my eyes and checked out my appearance. I had to admit that when I wasn't covered in an inch of dirt, I did manage to look half-decent. Dahlia had shaded my eyes with a pale pink to match my dress and painted my lips a nude pink. I looked at my face, and two golden-ringed irises looked back at me, reminding me that although I was the heir to the throne of Draconis, I was just as much an outsider as the fae man I'd seen earlier.

In all my travels, and I had traveled a lot, I was yet to come upon anyone who had eyes quite as unique as mine. Not even the amethyst-eyed faery I'd seen before was as unusual as I was in the eye department. I'd met a few fae in my time, and they often had jewel-colored eyes. Yes, they were rare and in the kingdom of Draconis, even rarer, but my eyes were the rarest of them all.

After pulling the dress over my head and having the bows

at the back fastened by Dahlia, my mother appeared at the door. She had also changed for the occasion...whatever it was.

As usual, she looked stunning, her beautiful golden hair tied back in a simple bow and a dress that was far less poufy than mine.

"Do I get to know who it is I'm meeting yet?" I asked, keenly aware that Dahlia was pressed up against me, almost as eager as I was to know what this was all about.

"Come with me," Mother said, taking my hand and ignoring my question entirely.

I followed her through the castle, the clack-clack-clack of her shoes echoing off the walls. She took me to the drawing room, the most comfortable room in the castle with pink upholstered chairs and beautiful tapestries hand-stitched by my mother hanging on the walls.

It was unusual to receive guests here. This was a room set aside for family only. My father stood to greet us as we walked in. He was still a handsome man, his dark hair showing the faintest signs of grey at the temples. The way his eyes lit up as my mother walked in the room made me slightly jealous. No one had ever looked at me as intently as my father did my mother every time he saw her. They'd been married eighteen years, and they were still like newlyweds.

I wished that one day, someone would look at me that way. No one usually noticed me at all if mother was around.

But someone did look at you that way only today!

A voice sounded in my head, but it was wrong. The faery had looked at me with intense eyes, but there had been no pleasure in them.

"Sit down Azia," my father asked gently, sneaking a quick reassuring glance at my mother.

Uh oh, this didn't bode well.

"This is important. You turned eighteen a while back, and

we both think that it's time for you to be more active in royal life."

Uh, huh. "I am active Father," I replied, finding a seat on the elegant couch next to my mother and trying to figure out a way to sit comfortably with all the layers of skirt beneath my ass. "I attend all the royal parties and come with you on all the royal travels."

My father nodded his head, his expression turning serious. "I understand that Azia, but being a queen is a whole lot more than trips and parties, and one day you will be queen. We are only one of twelve other kingdoms, thirteen if you include Urbis itself. Being the ruler of the kingdom requires a delicate balance of strength and diplomacy. As you know, I've been very fortunate during my reign; there has been peace in the kingdoms, but it wasn't always that way. Before I saved your mother, Draconis was in the grip of a terrible curse."

"But you saved her and the kingdom by kissing her." I knew the story by heart. It was famous. Even I, with not an ounce of romance in my bones, loved the story. The story of Sleeping Beauty and her brave prince.

"Yes," my father nodded his head, thoughtfully. "But the truth is, something else happened at that time. Something that, to this day, no one understands. I'm not so arrogant to believe that I saved your mother. I'm glad it was me, but the truth was, anyone could have gotten through the brambles to kiss her."

My mother put her hand on his arm in a gesture of love. "Don't be so modest, darling. It was true love's kiss that awoke me. No one but you could have done that."

He gave her a smile that made my heart melt, and my stomach heave in equal measures. It really should be illegal how mushy these two were for each other.

"Maybe," he agreed. "I know a lot of people had tried

before me, but why did I get through? Something happened at that time. It didn't just affect our kingdom. There had been widespread disquiet and war for years, and in the week I saved your mother, it was like all the bad in the world was vanquished. Anyway, I digress. Things have been very easy for me. It is always easy to reign when the people in the kingdom are happy, but things might not always be this way, and I need to prepare you for any eventuality."

"You want me to learn about ruling the kingdom?"

My heart took an unexpected leap in my chest. I'd been thinking about so many horrible things that could happen that I'd not prepared myself for something good. I wanted to learn more. I could never equal the level of beauty my mother possessed, but hopefully, I'd measure up in the strength and capability of my father. Before now, leading the kingdom had been something in the distant future, something I'd never been interested in, but now the possibilities seemed endless. One day, I would be queen of Draconis, and my parents were going to teach me how.

"Indeed I do,"

"Thank you, father!" I stood and kissed him on the cheek, but he brought me into a hug. As his warm arms wrapped around me, all my fears from earlier dissipated.

"So who was it you both wanted me to meet? A tutor of some kind?"

I saw a look pass between my mother and father as he let me go.

"Something like that."

Something like that? Uh, oh. What did that mean?

"I should go and see where he is," My father stood up, his finger and thumb rubbing together. "I don't believe he's arrived yet. Darling, could you go and organize tea?"

My mother couldn't have gotten up faster if she had tried. She hurried out of the door, pursued by my father, leaving me alone with my anxiety. This was no tutor I was meeting, so who was it, and why had my mother practically bolted for the door at the earliest opportunity?

I waited for ten whole minutes, nerves frayed. The lack of information on who I was to meet was crippling. Why the secrecy? When my father eventually came back through the door, my heart did a lap around my rib cage, but he was alone, his face set in a look of confusion. "I'm afraid there has been a mix-up. The gentleman I was going to introduce to you has not arrived. I'm sorry for getting you all dressed up for nothing, Azia. I know how much you hate all the pomp that goes with these things."

These things? What things? He'd still not told me what exactly we were doing. My mother chose this moment to come through the door, a loaded silver tray with a teapot and three cups on it.

When she saw my father, she adopted the same look of confusion. She placed the silver tray upon the table, then turned her attention to my father.

"Where is he?"

"I've just had word from a servant boy from the town that he is late and will see us tomorrow."

"That's very rude of him," my mother said. If there was anything she hated (apart from me being constantly covered in dirt), it was tardiness.

My father shrugged. "Can't be helped. You head off to bed now, Azia. I'll take a trip into town and see what happened."

I trudged back to my room, unsure of what to think. Both my parents were acting strangely, and neither was particularly forthcoming as to why. The room was dark, which was unusual. Dahlia usually left the candles burning for me. I walked to the window and opened the curtains to let a little moonlight in. A shiver ran down my spine as I caught the sound of someone else breathing and the feeling of being watched gripped me as intensely as it had out in the field earlier. Holding my own breath, I strained my ears to hear it, but there was only the sound of one of the guards coughing outside. I felt for the matches, gazing out into the courtyard as I did. It looked as it always did, lit only by a sliver of light from the crescent moon. Two guards stood by the portcullis, and as I watched them, one of them coughed again making me relax a little. Apart from the guards, the courtyard was empty.

"You won't find anyone of interest out there."

My heart lurched in my chest at the voice coming from behind me. Turning quickly, I let go of the window that slammed closed behind me. It was him! The faery I'd seen earlier was now sitting on my bed as if he owned the place. His devastating beauty captivated me, leaving me breathless despite the fact he held his sword aloft, aimed directly at my throat. This was no social call. He was here to slit my throat.

2ND JANUARY

"How did you get in here?" I whispered, my voice tense, my breathing ragged. Having a sword held to my throat was not something I usually enjoyed. Hell, I wasn't enjoying it now.

In the moonlight, he was more beautiful than ever, but that didn't stop the adrenaline rushing through me. My mind whirled as my fight or flight impulse stalled. I could run, but to do that I would have to run past him. Fighting was my only option. Unfortunately, he still had that beautiful sword in his hand, and I had no doubt he knew how to use it. My own sword was old, stolen months ago from the armory in the basement of the castle. My mother would have pitched a fit if she knew I had it, so I kept it under my bed. The bed that he was currently sitting on. The only other swords I owned were the trick swords I'd had made for Remy who wanted to learn to fight almost as much as I did. Fat lot of good they would be against the thing of beauty the faery held in his hand.

Talking of things of beauty, the fae's eyes danced in the little light there was, eyes that pierced me, pulling me in. He was utterly devastatingly gorgeous only spoiled slightly by the fact that it seemed he was here to kill me. That kinda thing could really put a dampener on any relationship.

Scanning the room quickly, I picked up the only thing currently in reach. The candlestick by my side. Pulling the unlit candles from the top of their holder, I held it out toward him as I would if I was holding a sword. Except it wasn't a sword. It had three holders on one end that held the candles and a stand at the bottom to stop it from toppling over. It was far from ideal, but it was long, and with luck, I could inch my way around him.

He watched me intently as I walked around the bed to the door, but he didn't move except to follow me with his sword. Instead, he studied my movements, watching me intently like a feline about to pounce, the line of his sword never wavering. My hand grasped the door handle at exactly the same time that his hand tightened on the hilt of his sword. He moved so quickly that I almost missed what was happening. The door handle turned, then stilled as a flash of light came down between the faery and me. My breathing increased as he moved his face to mine.

"This isn't quite the welcome I expected," he said, pinning my back to the door and holding his sword to my neck once again. His breath warmed my cheek, he was that close. I sucked in a breath of my own, trying not to lose it. He smelled faintly of wood and leather. He let his gaze fall down my body, and, all at once, I became aware that only the thin, gauzy fabric of my gown separated us. His tongue licked his lips as he took me in, holding me defenselessly to the door. Not that I could move if I'd have wanted to. There was something holding me back. Even if he didn't have his sword to my throat, my muscles had completely forgotten how to work, and the energy I'd felt earlier coursed through me. Not any energy. Fae magic.

My muscles tensed as he pulled my gown tightly enough to see the shape of my body, the curves of my breasts and hips. I followed his gaze to the floor, where the candleholder was lying uselessly in two pieces. His sword had cut through the metal like butter.

His energy was overwhelming, but I had to try to fight. I didn't know why he was here, and I wasn't prepared to find out. Pulling my leg back as far as I could, I put all the strength I had left into it, kicking forward until my knee connected with his leg. Not quite where I was aiming for, but it took him by surprise. He pulled back, and as his sword left my throat, I dove down to the floor and slithered to the bed where my own sword was hidden. Now, my sword was no match for his, but it was forged from the metal mined by the dwarves under the Fire Mountains, which meant it was strong and held a magic of its own, not that I knew how to embrace that magic. I'd never trained as a warrior the way Ash and Hollis had, but I'd watched them intently, copying their moves, practicing where no one could see me.

The intruder seemed surprised by the turn of events, but there was no fear in his eyes. If anything, he seemed to relish the challenge.

I lashed out at him, trying to quell my own fear. A shaking hand had no place in a sword fight, but play fights with Remy aside, this was my first. He swiped my sword away with mild irritation, the way one might swat a fly. He wasn't even trying, and yet, I was giving him everything I had. It was woefully obvious that I was no match for him. While I was trying every move I knew, he'd not even broken a sweat. At one point, I swear, the fae bastard yawned.

"Are we done yet?" he asked lazily. Before he'd uttered the last syllable, my sword vanished into thin air with a flick of his hand, leaving me with nothing to defend myself but the scream upon my lips.

I don't know why I hadn't thought of it earlier. Maybe I wasn't the swordswoman I thought I was, but there were two guards on the end of every corridor who did know how to sword fight. Two guards who would be here in a moment at the sound of my screams.

As he realized what I was about to do, the lazy attitude he'd shown moments before left him, and he rushed at me, knocking me over onto the bed, his hand clasped firmly over my mouth.

I breathed deeply through my nose, trying to fend off the rising panic at this crazy faery, lying directly on top of me. His eyes softened a bit, but he didn't take his hand from my mouth.

"Have you had your fun now?"

I glared at him, my stomach tightening as he pressed in closer, the weight of him crushing me. Up close, I saw that his eyes were framed by lashes so dark and thick that not even Dahlia with her extensive makeup knowledge would be able to recreate them. His skin was pale and flawless, and if it weren't for the amusement in his purple eyes, I'd have thought him made of marble.

"I'm not here to hurt you," he growled, "but with a welcome like that, I might change my mind."

I struggled against him, which only served to amuse him more. He pulled my arms up above my head, and I thought, for a second, he was going to kiss me. Let him try. I'd bite his tongue right out of his mouth. He didn't, though. He merely waited, watching me silently.

It took me a good few seconds to put my thoughts in order to speak to him, but I had to wait until he took his hand from my mouth to say anything.

"I can see you have something to say, but until you promise me that you won't do anything stupid such as scream or spit in my face, I won't take my hand away, do you understand?"

I nodded as much as I could with a hand over my mouth. He lessened his grip, and I breathed in, grateful of the cold night air.

"What the hell do you think you are?" I hissed.

He laughed. "What am I? I think you already know." He tipped his head slightly to the side, exposing one of his pointed ears. "I think the more pertinent question should be, who I am."

I wasn't in the mood for games, but as he still had my hands clasped together over my head and the weight of his body on top of me, I decided that playing along was my only option at this point.

"Fine," I muttered through gritted teeth. "Who are you?"

He sat up, pulling me with him so that we were next to each other on the bed. Every part of me wanted to run for the door, but as I'd already seen, it would be a pointless endeavor.

"I, my dear, am your fiancé."

My stomach tightened as I tried to take in his words. The guy was obviously deranged. My fiancé?

"Didn't your parents tell you? They have come to the conclusion that you are old enough to marry, and I am the person they picked." He leaned forward and spoke in a low voice. "Apparently, I'm quite a catch! I had hoped to get to know you before we were formally introduced, but I see you need a little time."

The magical energy had me pinned to the spot, and yet, he was quite obviously insane. I didn't have the first clue why he was in my room, but his explanation left me in no doubt that I wasn't safe. Pulling myself out of his magnetic grip, I ran for the door a second time. This time, it opened at the first try. Pulling the door open, I screamed down the corridor loudly. As they had been trained, the two guards came pelting down the corridor, their swords raised.

"There's someone in my room," I gasped, trying to keep the tears at bay. The two guards ran past me, but when I turned around, the faery had gone. The first guard, an older gentleman with a receding hairline that even his helmet couldn't hide, checked the bathroom while the younger one checked my closet and under the bed. I knew they wouldn't find anything. However the faery had gotten into the room, he'd obviously gone out the same way.

"I'm sorry. I must have had a nightmare." What else could I say? A crazy faery had somehow magicked himself into my room, held a sword to my throat, and told me I was to marry him? It sounded crazy to my own ears. The elder of the two, a gruff-looking man with way too much ear hair making up for the lack of it on his head, nodded, and I noticed a roll of his eyes as he left the room.

"Well, sorry for taking you away from your night of excitement guarding the corridor," I hissed under my breath. Heat rose to my cheeks as the younger guard answered me.

"Don't worry about Jack. He's a miserable old coot at the best of times."

I lowered my head. "I'm sorry. I shouldn't have said that. It was unkind, and you both really did help me."

"Hey, that's our job. I'm here to keep you safe."

I looked up into the kindest pair of brown eyes I'd ever seen set onto a handsome face.

He smiled. "Are you sure you are alright? I don't want to leave you upset like this."

After everything that had happened, I felt soothed by his presence, but I could no more have a guard spend the night in my room than a faery. "I'm perfectly fine. I feel a little foolish, actually."

The guard glanced around the room again as though he

thought I wasn't being honest with him. When he was satisfied there was no one in my room, he stepped outside. "I'm going to stand guard right outside the door tonight. If you need me, just call out, and I'll be in here in a flash."

He was so kind and concerned that the anxiety I'd been feeling fell away. If the faery did decide to come back, there was no doubt in my mind that the guard would be as helpless against him as I was. Maybe this guard was an amazing swordsman, but the faery had magic, and as I'd already seen, it was hard to fight magic without any of your own.

I thanked him, closing the door. Standing with my back to it, I could hear him settling down at the other side.

As I stepped forward, my foot stood on something sharp. As I looked down, something glinted in the light. Picking it up, I saw it was an amethyst from the faery's sword. Anger filled me. Who did he think he was to just come into my bedroom unannounced and scare me half to death? I gripped the small jewel tightly and stormed across the room, anger filling my every pore. Opening the window, I hurled it as far as I could. Satisfied that it was far away, I turned back to the bed. The dent where he'd lain on top of me was still there. In a fit of anger, I pulled the covers taught, before hopping into bed.

He was no longer there. The strange energy he exuded was long gone, but the fear he'd produced, still pulled at my nerves. I couldn't expect the guards to help me, but there was no way I was going to be defenseless anymore. Tomorrow I would stop playing at sword fighting and start learning it for real.

...

A noise at my door made me jump. My sword was gone, and the candlestick I'd tried defending myself with was in pieces on the floor. Once again, I was at the mercy of whoever was on the other side.

My heart calmed a bit when I heard the voice from the other side. It was the young guard from the night before.

"Your Highness. It is morning, and my shift is coming to an end. I didn't want to leave without knowing if you were alright."

A smile played on my lips. The poor guy had spent the night outside my room, standing to attention, waiting for an attack that never came while I'd slept in a comfy bed, and here he was asking if I was all right.

I opened the door. Immediately, his deep brown eyes crinkled at the side. Just peeking out from below his helmet, soft brown curls flanked his ears. A small smile crept over his face. "Are you ok?"

I smiled back. "I'm fine. Thank you for looking out for me. I'm sorry to have been a bother."

"No bother at all. It was a privilege. Milo Kelly at your service." He nodded his head, and after giving me a lingering look, he set off down the corridor. I half expected him to turn around and say something to me, but he didn't.

Back in my bedroom, I dressed quickly before Dahlia could come to do the job. I didn't want to talk to her about what had happened last night. It was probably better she didn't know. There was only one person I needed to speak with, and if I wasn't quick, I'd miss him for the day.

I found him saddling up his horse in the stables, ready to go out to wherever he needed to go.

"Father, I need to speak to you."

He pulled a fur cloak around his shoulders and hopped aboard Talia, his horse.

"I'm in rather a rush. Can it wait until tonight?"

I stepped in front of the horse, blocking his path. "Not really. I need to know who it was you wanted me to meet last night. Why all the secrecy?"

My father sighed, "I didn't want to tell you like this, but

your mother and I think it's time you settled down. I'm so very proud of you, my daughter, but you have your own ideas and plans; and while that is all well and good, it takes ambition and dedication to rule a kingdom. You are spirited, and that's what I love about you the most, but you need someone to guide you. To stand by your side. To help you on your journey."

I tapped my foot, getting more and more annoyed by the second. Why didn't he just come out and say it? That he had me promised to someone. Someone I'd never met before he'd somehow appeared in my bedroom in the middle of the night. I wasn't going to let my father off easily, though. I needed him to tell me outright what he'd planned.

"Who? Who do you want to guide me?"

He shifted in the saddle. "I really would have preferred to tell you this tonight with your mother."

"Tell me now," I demanded. I wasn't usually one to demand anything of my parents, but after having a stranger magic his way into my room, I'd changed my mind.

"Your mother and I think it's time you got married, and we've found someone who we think you'll like. He's not from Draconis, but he's a powerful man. Your mother tells me he's good-looking, though I wouldn't know about that sort of thing. I'm sure you'll like him."

"This man. Is he a fae by any chance?"

Now, my father really looked uncomfortable. "How did you...never mind. Yes, he is one of the fae. He's a powerful man."

"So you said. What if I don't want to marry him?" because I most certainly did not. I'd only just turned eighteen a few days ago. I didn't even want a boyfriend yet, let alone a husband and certainly not the kind of man that called my brother an idiot then snuck into my room in the middle of the night and threatened me.

"Why not give it a little time before making any hasty decisions? He's coming over for tea tonight. You'll get to meet him then. I'm sure you'll find him an agreeable sort of fellow."

Yeah, if you call holding a sword to my throat agreeable. I stepped back and let my father pass, frustration gripping me. Tears of anger spilled down my cheeks at the thought of what my parents were doing to me. Why had none of this been mentioned before now? I gritted my teeth. Dragon's breath, I really could go for a full-on tantrum, but what would be the point? My father was the king and what he said went.

I spent the day in my room, not wanting to talk to anyone.

My mother found me hours later, still in my bed. I'd spent the day reading and trying to pretend I didn't exist. At least, that way I wouldn't be forced to marry a faery jackass.

"What's the matter?" she asked, noticing the scowl on my face. My mother didn't like scowling, it gave people wrinkles.

"You loved my father when you married him," I stated it as fact. This was no question.

"Yes, of course. I still love him dearly."

"So why is it you are asking me to marry out of duty?" I huffed. "You didn't. I'm not ready for this, and I don't want it."

My mother sighed. Even that simple noise sounded beautiful like the pealing of bells or a breath of wind on a summer's day. "I see you have been talking to your father. Come with me, and I'll tell you our reasons." My mother opened the door to my bedroom and beckoned me out. "We are not doing this to you out of mere tradition. We are doing it to protect you."

"Protect me?"

"Azia, you are a bright young woman, and I know, in time, that you'll be perfect for the role of queen. I know that with a bit of schooling, you will run this kingdom beautifully with or without a husband."

"So why the arranged marriage then?" I asked, darting around her to the corridor outside.

She twisted her own wedding ring on her finger, a gesture she always made when she was nervous.

"I didn't want to tell you this, and it probably won't even mean anything to you, but in the past couple of days, a dragon has been spotted flying over the moorlands."

She stopped there as though that explained everything. It did not!

"So? What does a dragon have to do with marrying me off at the first available opportunity?" The dragons usually stuck to the mountaintops. I used to enjoy watching them as a kid. Their serene beauty belying their fierce nature. They never usually came down as far as the moorlands, but if it was just flying and not bothering anyone, who cared?

She sighed and held the wall next to her as if to steady herself. She looked tired, as though this had been going through her mind all last night. Bringing her hand up to her throat, she began. "Before Draconis was at peace, the whole twelve kingdoms were at war, and there was nothing anyone could do to stop it. Even the government in Urbis that oversaw all the laws in all the kingdoms couldn't stop what was happening. There was a lot of dark magic. For years, those people who used their magic for evil were doing pretty much anything they wanted. It was part of that black magic that sent me into a hundred-year sleep."

I knew all this. The stories of my mother's sleep and the kiss that ended it were legendary, but I still didn't understand what that had to do with dragons...or me. I kept silent, knowing there was no point interrupting her. She would tell me.

"It was horrible, and it had gone on for so long that most

people had no fight left. Dark magic weighs on you. It's like the worst kind of depression, but worse, because the people it affected didn't even know why they were depressed. No one was happy, and the people committing unspeakable acts were normal folk, turning to the dark out of fear, sadness, and desperation. Sadness creeps into your soul and burns it until you no longer feel, and it somehow becomes a part of who you are. It was like that in my youth and for a hundred years while I slept. In that time, the dragons came down from the mountains a lot. No one knows why. Maybe they were feeling the same things we were all feeling. The people in all the kingdoms were killing each other, so why not the dragons too? Like I said, a dragon has been seen down from the mountain for the first time since I married your father. It is an omen of the worst kind. You can't understand how awful it was. You could never imagine, because your whole life, you have only known peace."

A shiver of fear ran through me. My mother often told the story of how my father fought through a wall of brambles to kiss her, which woke her up, but she never talked about what happened before. I knew that an evil witch had cursed her and that the witch had gone long before my mother awoke, but she'd never mentioned the wars before and the dark magic. "I still don't understand. What has this to do with me getting married?"

She took my hand in hers. "Your father and I want to keep you safe. It was the kings and queens, the governors, the ministers, and presidents that were targeted before. I don't like to think that the same is happening again, but the man you are just about to meet is magic. He can protect you in ways that we can't."

He can protect me from outside dangers? So who was going to protect me from him?

"You want me to marry to keep me safe?"

She shook her head. "I don't really want you to marry, but if anything should happen to your father and me, I want to know you aren't alone. Remy will need care for the rest of his life, and Ash and Hollis are still children. You'll need help. You'll need someone who loves you by your side."

I sighed with frustration. There was no way the faery loved me. He'd only ever looked upon me with disdain and a hint of glee when he knew I was trapped. Hardly the recipe for a happy marriage. "The castle is full of advisors and men and woman who would step up in a heartbeat to help me rule a kingdom."

My mother nodded and took my hand in hers, and once again, we began to walk. "That is true. Our staff are some of the best, but unless they are family, this will never be any more than a job to them. Even our most loyal advisors leave the castle at the end of the day to go home to their own families. I cannot ask them to choose you or us over the ones they love. If you had a boyfriend already...that would be different, but you've never shown any interest in love."

We made it to the door to the drawing room. The man I was supposed to marry, the same one who had tried to kill me was inside. My mother had said that my father trusted him. I wondered how much he'd trust him if I told him where he was last night.

The fae was talking to my father as we walked in, but as soon as he heard us, his eyes turned to me. His hair was brushed back and the braids he wore tied behind. He wore some kind of ceremonial uniform. One I didn't recognize from any of the kingdoms. It was white with gold trim and amethyst colored buttons. He was off the charts beautiful. Even from across the room, he held me in his gaze. This wasn't attraction. There was no love nor chemistry between us. I didn't even like the guy, but right at that moment, I was drawn to him in a way I'd never been with anyone.

"There you both are." My father stood up and came over to me, breaking off my eye contact with the fae. Just like that, the spell was broken. The asshat had been using magic on me, some kind of attraction spell, and I'd very nearly fallen for it. What would have happened if my father had not blocked his path? It didn't bear thinking about.

"You both look beautiful," my father continued, kissing my cheek, before moving to kiss my mother.

"This is Caspian," he said, sitting back down. "Caspian, this is my daughter, the princess, Azia."

"Pleased to meet you, Azia." He stood and took my hand, kissing the back of it gently. A shiver went up my spine, whether through attraction or nerves or fear, I couldn't tell. Something was messing with my body... or someone was.

I pulled my hand from his. "It's very nice to meet you too," I answered through gritted teeth.

My mother busied herself with pouring tea into four cups, so I sat down, waiting to see what would happen next and wondering what I could do to drag myself out of this mess.

My father clasped his hands together and leaned forward in his chair. "We've been thinking of your future, Azia and..." He nodded to my mother as she handed him a cup of tea.

"She is aware of the reason Caspian is here," my mother butted in. "I've already explained the situation, and she is fully aware of what is going on.

"You're one lucky girl," Caspian said a smarmy smile on his face. Beneath it, I could still feel the disdain he held for me. If he despised me so much, what were we even doing here? What a sanctimonious creep.

My mother tugged my father's hand. "Now that everything is out in the open, why not leave these two alone to get to know one another? We can retire to the orangery and drink our tea there." She gave my father a meaningful look, and he stood, taking her hand, and following her from the room.

Clenching my jaw, I breathed deeply through my teeth. I was once again going to be alone in a room with this jerk.

I opened my mouth to say something, words to the effect of "no way," but nothing came out.

Casting my eyes to the fae, I saw him, once again, staring at me. When the door slammed shut behind my mother and father, my voice magically came back to me.

"Stop doing that," I demanded, my finger outstretched, anger coursing through me. He was a manipulator and a magical one to boot.

He sat back on the sofa as languidly as any cat and crossed his arms, a smirk painting his face.

"But it's so much fun. Why not sit down? I promise to keep my sword at my side."

My gaze wandered down to his sword, and I remembered with great satisfaction that he had lost an amethyst from its hilt the night before. It was beautiful, but flawed, a little like its owner.

"I'm not marrying you," I hissed. He continued to watch me as I threw myself down on a seat away from him.

"I really should apologize for last night. I'm not in the habit of coming into girls' rooms in the middle of the night."

"And sticking a sword to their throat," I added for him.

"Quite, it's just that I've been watching you, and you are not quite what I expected of a princess— Sleeping Beauty's daughter, no less."

"Sorry to disappoint," I shot back.

"No, actually I like it. I was expecting some kind of up herself prissy girl obsessed by her own looks, but you are almost beautiful without caring. It makes a refreshing change. I live in The Forge, and beauty is the currency there. It's extremely boring."

He was getting close to getting a teapot to the head if he continued talking. I picked up a teacup and held it so tightly I was afraid it might smash under the force. At least then, I'd have something sharp to gut him with if the need arose. The thought of stabbing him with a sharp piece of broken china calmed me down, enabling me to speak to him evenly without screaming.

"I'd rather marry literally any other man in the kingdom than you," I growled. "And that includes a troll I once saw living under a bridge."

He roared with laughter. "I've been training as a warrior for most of my life. You'll find your parents think I'm the best man for the job. The deal is, how do you say...done." His eyes centered on mine, and once again, I felt my body reacting to him. Damn it!

The way he looked at me made my heart pound and my stomach churn in equal measure, but my brain wanted to clock the guy right in the nose.

"Look. I don't know what magic you are performing on me, but it isn't going to work." The truth was, his magic was affecting me in ways I'd never imagined. I just didn't want him to know that. My pulse raced every time I looked at him.

"What makes you think I'm performing magic on you?"

Damn. He'd backed me into a proverbial corner. I could hardly tell him that just looking at him made me weak and dizzy....and sick.

"Just stop, all right?" I said, slamming the cup back on the table and standing up, turning away from him so I didn't have to look into his eyes a moment longer. "I'm sorry you have come such a long way to meet with me," I said calmly, measuring my words, "and I understand that you and my father are friends, but I'm afraid I cannot marry you."

"So you've said," the faery replied, sipping on his tea. "What you have failed to tell me is why not."

Because you are a jerk of epic proportions?

"Because I'm already dating someone else." What had made me say that? I wasn't dating anyone.

The door opened, and my mother and father came back into the room hand in hand.

"How is everyone doing?" my mother asked pleasantly, expectation plainly on her face.

Caspian answered for me. "Azia was just telling me she can't marry me because she is dating someone else."

He was annoyed. I could hear it in his voice. I preferred it to the smug drawl he'd used before. "I traveled a long way to be here, and I was assured that this was set to go ahead."

My mother and father's eyes swiveled towards me.

"You're dating?" My mother asked in a shaky soft voice. She dropped my father's hand and clutched her own to her chest. Probably because I'd not told her before. Not that there was anything to tell. I didn't know any men beyond the castle walls.

"Who is it Azia?" My father asked in a sigh. He didn't seem shocked in the way my mother was, but the look of annoyance on his face was evident. This was not the way they planned the evening to go, but then again, it was hardly my idea of fun either. They'd dropped a huge bombshell on me, so now I was giving them a taste of their own medicine. The only problem was I didn't have an answer to give.

I fumbled around in my mind, trying to come up with a name. Any name.

"Milo Kelly!" I blurted out. My mother and father looked at each other.

"Milo Kelly? Who's he?"

3RD JANUARY

"All this time, I've hoped you'd find a nice young man, and now, at the worst possible moment, you tell me you're dating?" my mother lamented at breakfast the next morning. "Why didn't you mention Milo before?"

I'd spent the previous evening searching the castle for Milo to give him the head's up while my parents argued over what was to be done with me and placating Caspian who was pissed off with my little announcement. Dating Milo wasn't helping their cause at all. He was a guard, and although he worked in the castle, it was unlikely that he knew how to run a kingdom. Not that it had been adequately explained to me how the fae knew how to run a kingdom either. Thankfully, my parents had packed him off back to the capital, hopefully never to be seen again. I'd not found Milo, and now, it was a race to see who would get to him first. Me or my mother.

"It's new, and I didn't want to embarrass him," I fumbled, hoping that would tame her desire to go looking for him. She wouldn't want to embarrass her staff.

My mother waved my answer away while Ash and Hollis

smirked. At sixteen and fifteen respectively, they both looked on the verge of becoming men, but their attitudes had a lot of catching up to do. The pair of them were enjoying this immensely.

"It's very unfortunate," my mother began. "You heard what your father said last night. We need someone to guide you. Someone who is a leader. Someone who..."

"Someone like me?"

My heart dropped as Caspian sauntered into the room, helping himself to a piece of toast and giving me a wink as he sat in the seat next to me.

My mother smiled at him, making me want to puke. I would have asked why he was here, but obviously, he'd not gone back to the capital as I thought. They'd invited him to stay. Dragon balls!

"Will you be with us much longer?" I inquired, trying to sound innocent and not in the murderous rage that I felt. "It's just a shame you've come so far and for nothing."

"I wouldn't say for nothing," he replied cryptically.

My mother buttered a piece of toast and passed it to him. "You may be dating this Milo fellow, but as you've said it's a new romance and most romances don't last," My mother said. "Caspian will be staying with us a while, and I'd like you to take some time to get to know him."

I shook my head in disbelief. "I don't want to get to know him. I'm dating Milo."

"Are you in love with Milo?" inquired Caspian. At the other side of the table, my mother watched curiously at what I was going to say. Ash and Hollis did the same. Only Remy continued eating his cornflakes like nothing important was going on. Turning back to the faery, I was ready to tell him that I was in the deepest love possible, but I could feel the tendrils of his magic poking at my mind.

"No. I barely know him," I said. Dragon balls! Why had I said that?

"Well, that settles it then. I'm sure your young man will get over it."

Mother, seemingly satisfied with my answer, shifted her focus back to her breakfast while I was left wondering what the hell just happened. Glancing over at the faery, he gave me a sly grin then poured himself a cup of coffee.

He'd made me say those words. He'd made me tell the truth. I'd been thinking it, but it hadn't been what I wanted to say. I hated him even more. It was bad enough that he crept into my room, but to mess with my own mind. That was other-level dragon crap.

"If you excuse me, I have to go and talk to Milo." I stood up from the table, throwing my napkin down in disgust.

"Let him down gently darling," my mother advised, giving me a knowing look. "Men are never very great when it comes to heartbreak."

Cursing the pair of them, I left the room, wondering how I was supposed to get myself out of this mess.

I wasn't going to marry Caspian, that was for sure, but I could hardly marry Milo either. For all I knew, he already was married. He probably had five kids at home. Searching the rest of the castle, I was forced to come to the conclusion that he wasn't at work today. I did, however, find the old guard he was working with the previous night.

"Have you seen Milo?"

The older guard narrowed his eyes. "He's not at work today. What do you want him for?"

I glared at him, and he quickly backed down. "I mean, is there anything I can help you with Your Highness?"

"Yes. Can you tell me where he lives? I need to see him."

The guard arched an eyebrow at this request, but I wasn't

about to tell him why I wanted to see his workmate. The guy obviously didn't like me...or his job.

"He lives in Zhore. Three doors down from the Dragon Roost Inn by the town square. It's a green house, can't miss it."

The capital city of Draconis, Zhore was actually our nearest town. I say town because it was barely big enough to qualify as a city. As most of Draconis was barren, the land didn't support a lot of people, so while we equaled in size most of the other kingdoms, we were vastly underpopulated compared to them. Luckily for me, the center of Zhore was just a thirty-minute walk away from the castle.

"And does he live with his wife?" I inquired, causing the old guard's eyebrows to shoot up once again.

"If Milo has a wife, he's yet to mention it," he huffed.

I thanked him and headed out of the castle. It was a beautiful day, which belied the squirming in my stomach. Remembering what my father had told me about the dragons, I cast my gaze to the tips of the Fire Mountains. A number of dragons circled the top as they did frequently, but none came lower, leading me to believe that my parents were worrying over nothing. I wasn't strictly allowed to walk into town by myself without a guard. But I figured, seeing as both my parents had succumbed to insanity at the moment, and technically, I was going to see a guard and would be with him part of the time, there was nothing they could say.

I pulled my hood over my head, shielding myself from the villagers. It rarely snowed in Draconis except on the tops of the Fire Mountains, but it was cold, and the hood would shield me from prying eyes.

The town square was a mess, debris left over from the celebrations on New Year's Eve. As I watched, a young boy with a cart swept up the discarded decorations and other detritus left from the celebrations.

I found the Dragon Roost Inn quickly, and from there, it was only a matter of looking for a house painted green.

The architecture in Draconis left a lot to be desired, and the ones here in Zhore were barely any better than the ones in the rest of the kingdom. What they lacked in quality and workmanship, they made up for in originality. As metal was in abundance and wood was scarce, many of the houses were built using a lot of it. Milo's house was no different in that respect. Built from brick, it featured a metal roof and doorway. Metal shutters painted green were clipped open on each side of all the windows creating a pleasing effect.

I raised my hand up to the wrought-iron knocker shaped like a face with a ring through its nose, but then paused. I'd been so eager to come here and talk to him, that I'd not spent any time thinking of exactly what I was going to say. I could hardly tell him that we were dating now. He'd think I was weird. Worse still, he might feel obligated to pretend for fear of losing his job. It wasn't I that employed him, but my father, and yet, the guards were all told to follow my orders too. How could I even think of asking him to go lie to my father? The whole thing was stupid, and yet to not do it would mean I had no excuse to get out of marrying the faery. My not wanting to, apparently, was not enough of a reason, and although my mother had waved off my fake budding romance with Milo as less than nothing, she couldn't ignore him if we were in love. Could she? I sighed and realized that this wasn't just my life I was playing with. I didn't know Milo, but he'd helped me at a time when I needed him. I couldn't bring all this on him. It wouldn't be fair. I was just about to turn away when the door opened.

I'd not even knocked.

"I saw you deliberating about knocking," Milo grinned at me. "You should come inside before anyone sees you. Are you here alone?"

He took my hand and pulled me inside, giving a quick glance up and down the street before closing the door behind me. His hands were warm, but he let go and dropped into a bow immediately after the door clicked into place. "Forgive me, Your Highness, for my rudeness. I just didn't like you being out there alone. It's not safe for you."

"Please stand. You weren't rude; I was. I'm sorry to have bothered you, I..." my train of thought wandered as I took in the sight behind him. The walls were lined with pieces of art, all made from metal. An abstract sculpture made of curves and swirls filled the far wall, reminding me of the ocean, even though it was static. One of the other walls had sculptures of animals, and a third wall held all manner of swords, each one more beautiful than the last. My breath caught in my throat as I saw a sword not unlike the Fae's sword, although it held rubies instead of amethysts. The hilt was shaped into a dragon, the rubies making up the eyes. It was exquisite, unlike the plain swords worn by the castle guards. I immediately felt a connection to it like no other sword. It made my own stolen sword look like a child's toy. I took my coat off and laid it on the arm of his sofa, not taking my eyes from the sword the whole time.

"This is beautiful. Where did you get it?" I whispered, moving across the room and bringing my hand up to touch it.

Milo pulled it from the wall. "I made it myself. Would you like to hold it?"

The moment I took the hilt into my hand and wrapped my fingers around the metal, I knew that this sword was meant to be mine. It fit my hand perfectly, and when I held it out, I felt a power I'd never known before. I was no longer Princess Azia of Draconis; I was a warrior. A warrior who could rule the kingdom alone, who didn't need anyone by her side, let alone the slimy fae.

I waved the sword, thrusting it forward slowly, defeating an invisible foe and causing Milo to jump back.

"You aren't holding it right," he said, coming up behind me and taking my hand at the wrist. "I've seen you practicing in the fields behind the castle." He adjusted my grip and the position of my hand. His warm breath tickled my ear, sending goose bumps down my arm. I'd barely been aware of him, but in this close proximity, the thrill of the sword was now overtaken by the feel of his body against mine.

He must have realized at the same time as I did because he jumped back and once again, dropped into a bow. "I'm so awfully sorry, Your Highness. I shouldn't have been so bold as to presume..."

"Please stop calling me Your Highness," I said, placing the sword back on the wall. I was reluctant to let it go, but it wasn't mine.

"My name is Azia, and it is I that should be apologizing. I shouldn't have come to your house. It could get you in trouble."

He looked up from his bow and stood up straight. "Trouble? I'm not scared of trouble, but I am interested as to why you would visit me."

My cheeks colored as I remembered the reason I'd come here. How could I tell him the truth? I couldn't. I'd have to figure a way to get it through to my parents that I wasn't marrying Caspian.

My brain whirred, but nothing came to me. "How much for the sword?" I asked, changing the subject instead.

It didn't matter how much he said. I was both rich, and I was poor. My parents had given me everything I could ever want, but there was no way they'd give me the money for this. Milo could give me a figure; I'd say thanks and then be on my way.

He walked back to the sword and once again took it from

the wall. He held it out to me. "The sword is yours. It is my pleasure to give it to you."

I stared at him, shock racing through me. As the daughter of a king, I was accustomed to being given gifts. Any trip to foreign kingdoms usually resulted in a carriage full of presents, but this was something else. Milo wasn't a rich diplomat or a member of the royalty. He was a guard who used his artistic gift to make things. The rubies alone would be worth a lot of money.

"I cannot accept this."

Milo thrust the sword into my hand. "I made this sword after watching you practice one evening. The sun glowed red, silhouetting you, and the dragons circled low in the air. You were so wrapped up in what you were doing that you didn't notice them, but I did. As soon as my shift ended, I ran home and designed this. It took a few days to make it, but you were the inspiration. If anyone is meant to have this sword, it is you."

His words were beautiful, and yet, something he said reminded me of my father's own words.

"The dragons were circling low? Lower than usual?"

Milo arched a brow, probably confused at the subject change. "Yes, but they were still far above you. You were in no danger. You were wearing a red and gold robe and looked like you were commanding them. You were the queen of the dragons that day."

I remembered the robe he was talking about. It was a present from my mother. I'd only worn it one time, on my birthday. Milo must have made this sword recently.

"That's beautiful," I whispered, "but I cannot accept such a gift from you. I don't even know you."

"So let's change that." He took the sword from my hand once again and placed it on the wall. "I'll keep this here until a time you decide you want it." He stepped back and held his hand out for me to shake. "My name is Milo. I've lived in Zhore my whole life. My father worked in the mines, and my mother made jewelry from the metal that came from them."

"Your father worked in the mines?"

He began to laugh. He must have understood my confusion. Only dwarves worked the Fire Mountain mines, and they were fiercely protective of them. Humans were not allowed in there. It was said that they imbued a spell into every piece of metal that no other magical person could break.

"He was an intermediary between the dwarves and the humans and was only allowed in the entrance to the mines, which the dwarves made into a shop. Even after twenty-five years of working there, he never ventured in any further. The dwarves needed food and such to survive, and they only had precious metals and stones. My father was a necessary evil as far as they were concerned, but they treated him well, and as you can see, we were never short of metal to work with. He loved his job. He told me stories of the dwarves all the time, how they used to complain about anything and everything. I think he found them funny, but he did his job well. He was the only human allowed to work in the mines until the day he died. They asked me to take his job, but I'd just been appointed at the castle, and I love my job."

"I'm sorry to hear about your father's death. What about your mother? Where is she?"

"When my father died, my mother realized that life was too short. She'd spent her life working the metals that my father had brought home into beautiful jewelry to sell to people at The Forge and other kingdoms. She'd saved up enough to travel, so she cut out the middleman, loaded up our family carriage with her jewelry and some of the swords I'd made and moved to The Forge. I hear she's living in a massive apartment there now, although some of her letters come from other places so I know she vacations a lot."

"It sounds wonderful," I said, noticing a clear box on a stand. Upon a red velvet cushion lay a beautiful ruby necklace. One of his mother's I assumed.

"She's enjoying life," Milo said, taking my attention from the necklace. "I might do the same thing when I've saved up enough, but there's not as much call for intricate swords here as there is for jewelry. The castle uses another supplier, and the guards use a basic design. It's cheaper that way."

"Yeah, they are nowhere near as pretty as yours, though."

Milo's face dropped. "I'm sorry. I didn't mean to offend the king. I wasn't calling him cheap. Getting the best price for swords in this climate is the better choice. I would have done the same if it were I. We live in peaceful times, and if I'm going to be honest, my swords are purchased more for decoration than for actual use, although you'll not find a stronger sword than the ones I make."

"Actually, my father thinks things are beginning to change," I sighed, sitting down on one of Milo's comfy couches. "He says that there is something in the air. You said yourself that the dragons were circling lower than normal. He thinks it's an omen of how things were before."

"Before he rescued your mother, you mean?" he asked, sitting beside me.

It figured he knew the story. Everyone knew the story. "Yeah. He thinks that he was only able to rescue her because the curse was already broken. I mean, so many other people tried to cut through those brambles before he did. Why did he get through when no one else could?"

Milo shrugged. "I don't know. My father told me that he had a line of people begging for the dwarves' metal every day for years, but when the brambles receded, people stopped coming. My father's workload cut by a half the day your father rescued your mother."

"Wow. I've only ever thought of the positives of that story. Did things get hard for your father then?"

He twisted on the couch, so he was facing more toward me. "Nah, he just tripled the price of the metals. People still came and bought it. It is magical to an extent, but those brambles had a strong curse, and even though swords made with the dwarves metal could cut through, they often grew just as quickly as they were cut, making it a pointless task to even try."

"Oh." Maybe my father was right, and he was lucky. Just what I needed, another thing to worry about. The dragons coming low in the sky was an omen according to my mother, but they'd done no damage, nor hurt anyone.

Milo must have seen the worry on my face because he scooted forward and laid a protective hand on my shoulder. "Listen. Don't worry about such things. I might have been exaggerating about the dragons. I don't really remember if they were lower in the sky than usual. They looked like they were, but it could have been a trick of the light or perspective."

I sighed. "I'm not really too worried about any curse or the dragons. I enjoy watching them. I find them beautiful."

"The queen of the dragons," he said again, smiling.

I laughed, feeling light for the first time since that jerk of a faery had turned up. It was nice to be with someone I could talk to away from the confines of the castle. The weight of the world was not as crippling as it had been just a few hours before.

"Not quite. I enjoy them from a distance...It's...It's my parents. They want me to marry someone I don't want to marry. They sprung it on me last night."

A look of comprehension dawned on him. "Ah, so that's why you are here. You are hiding from your parents."

I shook my head, dreading his reaction when I told him what I was about to tell him. "I wish that were the case. It's much worse than that. I told them I couldn't marry him because I was dating someone else, and in a panic, your name came to me."

Milo's mouth twisted into a grin. "Are you telling me that the king and queen think we are dating?"

He lounged back on his sofa, as my cheeks once again reddened. Dragon's breath, this was embarrassing. I'd been so worried about embarrassing him, that I'd not put any thought into how embarrassing this would be for me. And it was. My cheeks were hotter than a dragon's flame.

"Maybe," I admitted. "Just a little. My mother wants me to break up with you."

"No way!" He clasped his hands to his chest theatrically. "I love you too much. You are my heart, my soul, my one true love." He pulled me from the sofa and spun me around the room as though we were at a royal ball. He was teasing me, of course, using the same line that had become famous when my father kissed my mother, awakening her from her long sleep. She'd said at the time he was her one true love and that it had been love's true kiss that had awakened her.

"Stop it," I admonished, laughing at the moment of silliness. We were no longer princess and guard. We were just two people having fun. It was embarrassing sure, but it was fun too. I'd never done anything like this before. Such behavior was not acceptable at the castle.

"You know, this calls for a drink," He picked up the coat I'd left on the arm of the sofa and threw it at me. "Put your hood back on, we're going out."

I'd barely had time to cover my head when he took my hand and led me outside. It had gotten considerably darker, even though it wasn't even dinnertime yet. The bright skies I'd walked to town in were now filled with ominous dark clouds.

Milo noticed it too. "Looks like a storm is coming, but we have time for one drink. I'll walk you home after that. What do you say?"

Looking at the clouds, I guessed his estimate was wrong. The storm was almost upon us, but I'd rather walk home in the rain with him than through the dark streets without him. That way, if my mother caught me, I could tell her I'd been out on a date with Milo. She'd be more upset that I hadn't broken up with him than me wandering through the streets by myself.

The inside of the Dragon Roost Inn was darker than the thick clouds outside, making it clear that I wouldn't be recognized. I'd be surprised if anyone would see me at all. All I could see were various outlines of the customers.

"What do you want?"

I shrugged. I'd never been in a bar before, and the only alcoholic drink I'd ever partaken in was champagne at royal parties. "I don't even know what to order. You choose for me."

He left me in a booth and headed to the bar. It was quiet enough that he was served right away. The barmaid, a pretty woman with big hair and a slim waist, leaned forward. "Hi, Milo. What can I get you?"

"I'll have two beers, please. One for me and one for my friend."

The barmaid turned toward me, and I smiled, although I wasn't sure she'd even see my smile through the gloom, so I waved. She gave me half a smile back before her expression turned like milk gone sour. "Sure. I'll have to bring a keg up though."

I allowed myself a small grin. The poor barmaid was

probably crushing on Milo, and here he was with a girl. I wondered how she'd feel if she recognized me as the princess.

I waited in the booth while Milo stood at the bar. Another man took the seat next to him and began a conversation. He talked much more quietly than the barmaid had, but my ears were keen, and I picked up the gist of the conversation.

"Who's the girl, Milo? I thought you were holding out for the princess?" The old man laughed, and I blushed. Milo was holding out for me? He liked me? No wonder he hadn't been angry when I'd told him what I'd said to my mother. Dragon balls. That complicated matters. I liked Milo. He was fun, and yeah, he was cute, but I didn't need a boyfriend. I didn't want one. I wanted to learn who I was before I even thought of sharing my life with someone else. That was the point of this whole endeavor in the first place.

The old man's words didn't seem to faze Milo, though. "It's my new girlfriend. I'd take you over to introduce you, but I wouldn't want to put her off her beer."

Dragon crap! Now he was introducing me as his girlfriend.

The old man laughed again as a flash of lightning struck, lighting the bar for a brief second. I almost screamed as the face of an old woman was illuminated in front of me. A woman with thick wrinkles and barely any teeth. The pub fell into darkness, but the woman was still there, standing just inches from me.

"You are new here," she cackled. "I've never seen you before."

I tried to catch Milo's attention, but he was deep in conversation with his friend.

"I'm visiting someone," I said, pointing to Milo, hoping she'd get the hint and go away. She was very short, owing probably to the fact that she was hunched right over. There was nothing innately scary about her, but she put me on edge. A shiver ran down my back as she pointed a spindly finger at me.

"You are a woman of great power, but I don't think you know it. You parents. Who are they, Dearie?"

I tried to come up with a lie. She obviously didn't recognize me as the princess any more than Milo's friend or the barmaid had. I was spared having to pull something out of the air as she didn't wait for me to answer.

"Yes. I can see the power in you. It is like nothing I've ever seen before. Those eyes of yours—beautiful, but strange. I wonder if you see the power in yourself? You have a lot of hardship coming up young lady, but I don't doubt you'll fight it. There's something else I see in you, but I can't get a full picture. It's like you are not fully there. There's a lot of you missing. Scattered like leaves in the wind." The crash of thunder shut her up, and then thankfully, Milo returned with two beers in his hands.

He handed one to me. I glanced back up at the old woman, but she was already gone, slipping back into the gloom as quietly as she had appeared.

"Did you see her?" I asked Milo, shivering. He must have walked right past her.

He turned his head to look around the bar. "See who?"

How could he have not seen her? She'd been right next to me when he slipped into the booth opposite me.

"There was an old lady with a hunch back. She said that I'd have a lot of hardship and that part of me was missing."

"You look fully intact to me," he said good-naturedly, taking a sip of his beer. "It sounds like Gladys. She's crazy but harmless. She seems to think she can predict the future and makes a little cash, but she's a phony. Don't worry about her."

I took a sip of the beer. It tasted like nothing I'd ever tasted before. The cold liquid ran down my throat almost making me forget the old woman's words, but part of what she'd said resonated with me. I'd never felt whole. I'd been loved my whole life. By my parents, my siblings. Even the public kinda, sorta loved me when my mother wasn't around to adore, but I'd always felt that there was something missing. It was probably to do with me being adopted. I guessed most adopted kids felt that way at some time or another, but it was more than that. It was like part of my entire being was ripped away from me. The old woman had hit the nail on the head. I didn't feel whole. I'd never felt that way.

Milo placed his beer down on the table and flipped a beer mat, catching it back in his hand. "I don't often come in here, but occasionally, I'll come in for a drink. What do you think of it?" Milo asked me.

"It's very dark," I observed. "And the barmaid has a crush on you." I left out the part where his friend had mentioned him having a crush on me and the part where I'd overheard him calling me his girlfriend. It was a conversation I was going to have to have with him, but now was not the time.

He spluttered a bit then regained his composure. "Lisa doesn't have a crush on me!"

I glanced over at the barmaid who was very plainly staring at us, her elbow on the bar, supporting her head in her hands. When she saw me looking, she stuck her tongue out and moved away to tend the bar at the other side.

"Really?" My mouth curved up to the side.

Milo raised his hands in the air in mock surrender. "What can I say? I'm irresistible."

Lightning flashed again, illuminating his face. He really was cute with his deep brown eyes and curly brown hair. Freckles dotting the bridge of his nose. In another life, he was someone I could consider as a boyfriend. If I wanted a boyfriend, which I didn't.

"So let's talk about this great love affair we are supposedly having?" he said, his head resting on his hands. "Who asked who out? Have we kissed yet? You know I just told my friend you were my girlfriend. I figured we may as well start the ruse now."

"Oh, Dragon's breath! Don't. It's embarrassing. I'm sorry I ever told you." I was glad of the dark covering the grin on my face. At least, he was honest about telling the old guy I was his girlfriend. It had put my hackles up, but he was just having fun with it...hopefully.

"I'm not. This could be fun."

Yep. Fun. That's what it was.

"You know my mother wants me to break up with you," I said, leaning in closer. "She'll come looking for you, and knowing her, she will warn you off."

A mischievous grin appeared on his face, and as he spoke, he raised an eyebrow. "We should have one last torrid night of passion before we break up then."

"You wish!" I grinned back at him, trying not to laugh. I was having so much fun. No one ever spoke to me this way. I was used to decorum and rules. Drinking beer and talking about torrid nights of passion didn't feature heavily in my daily life.

"I'm engaged to another man," I reminded him. "Or at least, I would be if it weren't for you."

He shrugged as if this piece of information was inconsequential. "So what? You aren't married yet. Let's go back to the castle. I'll tell your mother how you broke my heart into a million pieces and that I cannot live without you."

"You should," I agreed. "She'll probably feel so guilty that she'll find a job for you in another house and send you on your way with a lot of money in your pockets."

We both sobered up at my words. My mother would fire him. She'd have to. She couldn't have an old flame of mine working in the castle while I was engaged to someone else.

"I'm sorry," I continued. "I'd not thought of that before. I won't let her fire you. I'll tell her that it was something and nothing and that we are completely over. I won't give her reason to sack you."

"So you don't want me to tell her about our torrid last night together then?" he asked, picking up his beer again and taking a sip. He left a white mustache of white foam behind on his upper lip.

"Maybe you could keep down the theatrics a little," I grinned at him, moving forward, and wiping the foam off with my thumb. His eyes locked on to mine as I held my thumb up.

"Foam," I explained.

No. I wouldn't let my mother fire him. I'd play down the romance and try to make her see sense about the faery.

I finished my beer, which went right to my head, making me a little woozy. I wasn't used to drinking much at all. The champagne I did get was measured in such small glasses that I usually only got a sip of two. Now, I'd downed a whole pint of the amber stuff.

I opened my mouth to tell him that our romance was only for show and that I didn't want to date him...or anyone else, but a peal of thunder hid my words.

Outside, someone screamed, making me forget what it was I was about to say.

Milo stood quickly, taking my hand in his as all around us, people left their seats to see what was going on. We both ran outside into the street as a dragon shot a breath of fire straight at us. Milo shut the door just in time before we both got barbecued.

My father had been right. The curse was returning. The dragons were back.

4TH JANUARY

I woke up to an urgent knocking on the door. Opening up my eyes, I tried to get my bearings in the unfamiliar room. Next to the bed, a side table held a book about ancient swords. It was a book I would have liked to have thumbed through, but it wasn't mine. Outside the room, another door opened, and then Milo spoke. He wasn't speaking particularly loudly, but just like in the bar, I could hear every word. My hearing was becoming keener with each passing day, though I didn't understand why.

"She's here. She's safe. I'll go get her."

Heavy footsteps sounded, getting closer, and then the door to the room flew open. Pulling the covers up to my neck, my muscles tensed as I recognized the man entering the room.

"Father!"

"Get out of bed!" he ordered, through gritted teeth, his red face scrunched in anger, "Now!"

I'd never seen my father look so angry in his whole life. His knuckles were white where he held his sword, his cape saturated by rain.

When I'd pulled myself from the warmth of Milo's bed, he pointed to the front door of Milo's house, leaving no room for misunderstanding.

"You," he shouted at Milo as we passed. "Get your ass up to the castle. If you don't have a horse, one of the guards will take you." He nodded to one of the castle guards who grabbed Milo's arm and began to drag him to the door.

Outside, wind blew torrential rain right into my face, making it difficult to see. The storm of last night was still going strong. I was almost pushed into the black carriage, and when the doors were closed, I was finally able to speak.

"This isn't what it looks like, Daddy," I said, reverting back to the name I'd called him as a child.

"I'll tell you what it looks like," he bellowed, slamming the curtains of the carriage shut. "While the dragons were rampaging through Zhore, you were here with some strange man. Sleeping in his bed, no less! Your mother is so unwell over the stress that she's been ordered to go to bed by the court physicians."

My mother was unwell? I knew staying out would have worried her, but I didn't want to hurt her.

"I'm sorry, Father. I was only in town to talk to Milo. Mother asked me to break up with him and..."

My father grimaced and drummed his fingers on his knee. "Talk? In his bed? Please, Azia. It didn't look like you were breaking up with him to me. I wasn't born yesterday."

"But I..."

"Save it for when we get home. I'm in no mood to talk to you right now. I've been out all night knocking on doors looking for you. I thought you'd been taken. That's what they did, you know. The dragons. They took people. Young girls were their favorite."

My heart dropped. Of course, he would come to that conclusion. "I'm sorry, Daddy."

He huffed and turned away from me.

We made the rest of the journey in silence, anxiety eating me up all the way. I wanted to know everything about the dragons, such as, if my father knew why they had come down from the mountains and if anyone was hurt. I had to be patient and wait, and all the time, I knew Milo was behind us on horseback, being forced to come with us.

I tapped my toe against the carriage floor as the anxiety of the situation threatened to take over. My father must have been aware of it, but he didn't say a word. Maybe he couldn't hear it over the staccato beat of the pouring rain hitting the carriage windows. After what seemed like an age, we arrived at the castle. The portcullis shut behind us, only letting the guards through, though I couldn't say why. If the dragons were still active, it would be easy for them to swoop into the open courtyard. As it was, we only had the rain to contend with as we trooped from the carriage to the castle entrance hall. I followed my father, and behind me, Milo was brought in flanked by two other guards.

"Father, please let him go," I begged. "He's done nothing wrong. He was protecting me; that's all."

"Is this the young man you spoke of yesterday?" My mother's voice drifted across the hall. I turned to her, and my heart lurched. My father had said she was ill, but nothing had prepared me for the sight of her. Her usually flawless face was marred with blotchy skin, and dark circles painted the skin under her eyes. Her usually perfect hair resembled a bird's nest, something that I'd never seen once, and she looked about to pass out. I ran to her, afraid she might fall without assistance.

"You should be in bed," my father said, taking her other arm. She swayed a little in his arms.

"I couldn't go to bed knowing Azia was outside. I'm just tired; that's all. Thank you for bringing my girl home."

A tear fell from her bloodshot eyes, and she brought us both in for a hug. This was more disconcerting than the blotchy face. My mother never lost it in front of people, and as far as I could tell, half the guards were currently in the entrance hall, most of them with swords trained on Milo.

"Sorry to interrupt your majesties, but can someone tell me why my lad Milo here, has fifteen swords at his belly?"

I turned to see the grouchy older guard, who worked alongside Milo. Jack, somebody. He didn't hide the irritation of having his workmate held up.

"I found Azia in his bed," my father announced, both to the guard and to my mother, making my cheeks flame once again.

"So bloody what?" Jack said. A round of titters went round the assembled guards. I'd never been so embarrassed in my whole life. And if my nonexistent love life being blown completely out of context wasn't bad enough, Caspian walked into the room, eating an apple.

"My fiancé has been sleeping with whom?" he inquired, not seeming particularly bothered by the current state of affairs. He wasn't angry, not that he had any right to be, merely curious.

"I've not been sleeping with anyone," I shouted out. "I went into town to see Milo. Mother, you already know we are dating. I was barely with him an hour when the dragons came down. They were spitting fire. Milo very kindly let me sleep at his house until the threat passed. I knew you would be worried for me, but I had no way of letting you know I was safe. I could hardly send a message to you and risk the life of someone. I had to do what everyone else in Zhore did yesterday. I hid." My throat constricted as I spoke, and I was aware that everyone was watching. "And yes, I slept in Milo's bed, but as you saw yourself, Father, when you barged through his door, he wasn't in it. He slept on the sofa all night. He was a perfect gentleman. Now could you please let him go!"

My voice had risen by at least an octave, and I was bordering on hysteria. The whole scene must have looked a sight to any outsiders.

My mother obviously thought the same thing. "Guards, leave the poor boy alone and go and do your jobs. There's enough to do at the moment without holding one of our own up. Alec, did you order this?"

My father looked down at the floor, shame written on his face. My usual stoic father was certainly running the gamut of emotions today. Not that I could blame him. There was a lot going on. He'd certainly never treated me the way he had this morning before. It just wasn't like him, but the strain in his voice was evident with every word he spoke.

"I was worried," he said, turning to me. "I am worried about both of you. Azia, please forgive me. I'm under a lot of stress. The kingdom is going to rack and ruin today, and I acted rashly." He lifted his hand to his brow and began to massage his temples.

I moved closer to him and lowered my voice." It's ok, Father, but I think you are apologizing to the wrong person." I moved my eyes to the retreating guards.

Milo was the only guard in the entrance hall not moving.

My father turned to him. "Young man, please accept my most humble apologies." He held his hand out, which Milo stood forward to accept. It was a great honor to shake the hand of the king, and yet, Milo did it with grace.

"Perhaps we should all sit down and have a talk about everything that's going on," my mother said.

"Milo, please be our guest, and Caspian, you'll join us for tea?"

"Delighted," he purred, giving me a wink, which brought a

bitter taste to my mouth. I was close to socking the guy in the face, but I held back. I was a princess, after all.

"I'll go and fetch Milo a towel," I offered, more to get away from Caspian's gaze than anything else. "He's soaked."

Milo followed me to the guest bathroom, and surprisingly, nobody stopped him.

I pulled a white towel embroidered with the castle crest from the cupboard and turned, ready to dry his hair.

He stood there in nothing but underwear, his almost naked body damp from the rain.

My heart pounded against my ribs, and my eyes widened at the sight of him. He was gorgeous. Because he had a cute face and curly hair, I'd not thought of him as someone to have such an amazing muscular body, but clearly, I was wrong. I cleared my throat, pulling the towel to my chest, trying to hide both the flush that was rising up my neck and my heart that seemed to be making an escape for freedom.

"I was going to dry your hair," I choked out.

He took a step closer and bent his head forward a little. If either my mother or my father walked in now, they would both ground me for a month, and Milo would lose his job. It would be pointless pretending this was all innocent when he was mostly naked, and I was rubbing my hands all over his body...his hair. I corrected my internal voice and pulled the towel over his head, trying to ignore the fact that below it, he had no clothes on except his underwear.

If Caspian walked in now, well, that would be another thing entirely. I'd get great satisfaction from seeing his face.

I rubbed Milo's hair vigorously, trying not to let this get any more intimate than it already was. I was already imagining the headlines in tomorrow's newspaper if we got caught. The dragons wouldn't get a mention. Besides, I reminded myself. I wasn't actually dating Milo nor did I want to. I wanted my freedom. Although, I could be persuaded to change my mind given the current situation.

I felt a tug and the towel came away from my hands. Milo quickly wiped down his body and made to get back into his saturated clothes.

"I think we may have a spare uniform. If you like, I can get it for you?" Yeah, please put clothes on before I do something stupid...like drool.

He looked up and gave me a smile. "That would be great, thank you."

When I hadn't moved, he raised his eyebrows.

Now was the time to tell him that I didn't want to date him in real life. Now was the time to mention that I only wanted him for show, for pretend to get out of marrying Caspian. It was unfair to him if he had a crush on me. If he knew that I wasn't ready to date in real life, then he could make up his own mind about whether to carry on the pretense. Now was the time...but he was so breathtaking that I couldn't get the words out.

I left the room and grabbed him a uniform from the storage cupboard off from the entrance hall. I was just about to pass it through the door to him when my mother caught up with me.

"Is Milo in there?"

I nodded, hoping that she wouldn't decide to go in herself to check up on him. Although, knowing my mother, she'd enjoy the display.

"Wonderful," she gave me a smile. "We are in the drawing room. Tell Milo to join us when he's ready."

I passed Milo the uniform through the door and headed to the drawing room, followed a minute or so later by Milo. He looked very handsome in his uniform. He took a seat next to me and took my hand in his, making me squirm. My mother noticed the gesture and pursed her lips, but she made no mention of it. I guess we had bigger fish to fry what with the dragon situation and all.

"Please excuse me," she said, nodding at Milo and trying to pull her hair back into something more presentable. "I was up all night. We have two major problems here. The dragons that affect all of us, including pretty much everyone in the kingdom, and the matter of Azia. That is why I wanted all parties involved here to discuss the matter. As one matter has directly arisen from another matter, I think we should discuss the dragons first. Milo and Caspian, normally, I wouldn't involve anyone outside of family in talks like this. They should be held between my husband and his advisors, but nothing is normal at the moment, and quite frankly, I think the king's advisors are running scared."

"I agree," my father said. "The dragons are definitely a problem we need to address first."

"Was anyone hurt, Your Majesty?" Milo asked. He leaned forward, resting his arms on his knees, showing great interest. By contrast, Caspian sat back and stared out of the window.

My father shook his head as he answered Milo. "No major casualties that I'm aware of, although I'm told there were a number of minor injuries from people tripping over themselves while running away. No one got burned, but I believe luck was involved. Now that the dragons are coming down the mountains, we will have to prepare."

I thought of the dragons that had been peaceful my whole life. Nothing about their sudden appearance made sense to me. Before yesterday I couldn't comprehend the thought of them causing havoc. They were such beautiful creatures, and if I was going to be honest with myself, I envied the way they lived, flying freely over the mountains. Many times throughout my childhood, I'd dreamed of being able to fly with them.

"How do we do that?" Caspian asked lazily. He didn't care one iota that dragons had invaded. He could scoot on back to The Forge whenever he wanted. I only wished he would.

My father put his head in his hands. I'd never seen him look so defeated before. He'd always spoken about how lucky he was to have never had to deal with any big problems during his reign. This was the first time he'd had to prove that he was the man in charge. Unfortunately, from where I was sitting, it looked like he was crumbling. Worry over my mother and then me only compounded everything, hitting him all at once. Without waiting for an answer, I spoke up.

"We need to set up some kind of alert system. A siren or something that could go off whenever a dragon is spotted lower down in the mountains."

My father shook his head. "That's all well and good, but the dragons are not really the main concern.

Before you were born...just before you were born, a reign of terror ended. Everyone over the age of twenty-five or so remembers how awful it was. The dragons were an omen. I can deal with them. I have an army that can go out and kill them all if need be. My men are trained in the art of combat. It's what's coming next that worries me."

The thought of my father's army killing all the dragons brought a lump to my throat. Yeah, they'd rampaged through the capital, but no one had been hurt. Before that, they'd kept to themselves, living peacefully in the mountains.

"Do you really believe that this is an omen?" I asked. I didn't believe in omens, and before this, my father had never been superstitious.

"Don't you feel it?" My father asked, directing his question to all of us in the room. "Something has changed. I can't describe it, but it's like nothing is quite right anymore."

Milo looked at me, and I shrugged.

"He's right," Caspian said, inspecting his nails. "There's

been a huge magical energy shift. I'm surprised you felt it as a mere human, Alec."

My father flinched at Caspian's choice of words. Mere human! Who did he think he was talking to?

"I think it was just about time for something to happen," Milo said, diffusing the situation. "It is a blip, and that is all. If you find a way to deal with the dragons, everything will go back to normal."

"Actually," Caspian jumped in. "I cannot disagree more, Mikey. I'm a magic-user, and because of that, I can sense that the vibrations in the air are off. I cannot tell what has caused the shift, but recently, as recently as last week, there was an event that happened, changing the magical atmosphere. I don't know what it was, but there was a massive shift in the magical equilibrium, and I think it will be a mistake to discount it."

"It's Milo," Milo corrected him.

"Hmmm," Caspian replied, unbothered by his deliberate mistake.

Ignoring the fae's rudeness, I thought back to the past week or so. It had been a great week, and nothing about it predicted doom and gloom, as far as I was concerned. First, there was Christmas where we opened the castle grounds for people to join us to celebrate. After that, came my eighteenth birthday, which was mainly spent eating cake and opening presents and, finally, the huge celebration ball we hosted every year for New Year's Eve. No doom and gloom here, just parties and fun. Caspian had to be wrong. He was a manipulator at the best of times, and this was far from that.

"Let's just see how this plays out," I argued. "It could be something and nothing. For all we know, someone decided to climb the Fire Mountains and steal a dragon egg. That would set the dragons off, right?"

"That would be an excessively stupid thing to do," my

father remarked, and beside him, my mother nodded her head.

"Yes," I agreed. "It would, but since when were people not stupid? We do stupid stuff all the time."

I purposefully looked at Caspian as I said this, but he'd gone back to gazing out of the window. I wondered for a second if I'd get away with throwing him through it.

My mother stood up, taking the floor between us. My father watched her like a hawk, ready to jump up and catch her in case she fell.

It warmed my heart. If I could guarantee a love like that, I might actually consider marriage. Not to Caspian, but to someone. My eyes caught Milo's and I looked down, worried he'd somehow catch my thoughts.

"The dragons have been coming down the mountain for a while," she said. "Last week, it was over the moorlands; last night, a couple of them rampaged through Zhore. What we don't know is why.

My father answered her. "Historical evidence suggests that it is an omen. Dragons hold a kind of magic that we humans know little about. They have only been known to come down the mountains in times of great stress."

"But it's the dragons causing the stress," Milo pointed out. "Apart from the two instances of them flying low, has anything else happened that could make you think that they are an omen?"

My mother held a hand to her head. "No. Nothing else has been reported. We could treat these as isolated incidents. Maybe, as Azia said earlier, someone was foolish enough to climb the mountains and disrupt them, but for the time being, we all need to be alert and prepare ourselves for the worst."

"I'll get my best men working on a solution to the problem," my father added, standing up to move nearer my mother. He picked up a glass of water and passed it to her. "I'll get them to ask around and see if they have seen anyone trying to sell dragon eggs. As you all are probably aware, the sale of dragon eggs is highly illegal, but that only drives their value up. It is definitely conceivable that someone decided to flout the law to make some money."

"That seems the best option at the moment, Alec, thank you." She took a sip of the water. "Which brings me to the next matter. Azia, I love you. You are my only daughter, and I want more than anything for you to be happy. However..."—she turned to Milo—"and this is no reflection on you, Milo." Turning back to me. "You cannot marry a guard. I took the initiative to look at his records. He's only been a guard for us for seven months. Probation and training last a year. He is not qualified to run a kingdom. I need someone by your side who can protect you. If he'd completed a little more training, maybe we could consider it."

"I've trained my whole life in swordsmanship, Your Majesty," Milo said. "My father made swords using metal from the mines, and I followed in his footsteps. As well as making them, I learned how to use them."

"Keeping a kingdom safe is not going to be helped by one man with a sword," Caspian uttered dismissively, waving a hand in the air. "A leader has to know how to protect all his subjects, not just the ones he lives with."

"With respect, sir," batted Milo back to him. "I wouldn't think of Azia and her brothers as my subjects if I married her. I'd think of them as family."

Caspian narrowed his eyes, and I could see that the conversation was ruffling his feathers. Good! He deserved it.

"It's the same thing when you are in charge," hissed Caspian.

"He called Remy an Idiot!" I shouted, adding to the argument. “He held a sword to my throat!"

My mother stood in the middle, clutching her ears.

"Enough!" she shouted. "This is just like this last time. People fighting over nothing. It doesn't matter about who is wrong or right in this particular argument. Azia cannot marry a castle guard, and that is final. I'm sorry."

"And I'm sorry," Caspian said, the smug look firmly back on his face. "I didn't mean to be offensive to your son."

I noticed he didn't apologize for what he'd done to me.

"Get out!" she yelled at him. I'd never seen her lose it like she was doing. Caspian stood and gave her a brief nod before walking past her and heading out the door. It would have been a moment of celebration if my mother hadn't chosen that moment to fall to the floor. Both Milo and my father moved to catch her.

"I'm fine, really," she whispered as my father took hold of her and pulled her back into a standing position. "I'm just so tired."

My father and Milo each took an arm, and between them, they helped her out of the room and up to her bed, leaving me alone in the drawing room.

She'd screamed at Caspian, which was good, but she'd also said I couldn't marry Milo, which was bad...kinda. I had no intention of marrying Milo any more than I had of marrying Caspian, but if my mother had forbidden it, surely that meant I still had to marry Caspian. It didn't bear thinking about.

As I pondered over the subject in my head, I moved over to the window and gazed out as I had done many times in my youth. Looking up, I spotted one or two dragons up by the snowy peaks of the tallest of the mountains. Up there, they looked serene, nothing like the ferocious beast with blazing red scales and a yellow underbelly that had blazed Zhore the night before. It had flown so close to me. Close enough that if I'd wanted to, I could have reached out and touched the tip of its wing. Once it had passed, Milo had taken my hand and rushed me back to his house.

The sound of the door opening again had me turning my head.

"Your mother is asleep," Milo said, standing by the door. He looked at me with a sheepish grin. "I'm sorry our plan didn't work. For what it was worth, I liked being your boyfriend for the past day, and it would have been the greatest honor to marry you."

"It's probably for the best," I sighed. "I've had so much fun with you, and I like you a lot, but I'm not ready to have a boyfriend. I want to see things, explore. I want to know who I am before I share myself with someone else."

"I can understand that," Milo said, taking a seat on the sofa. He picked up one of the untouched biscuits that my mother had brought in and began to chew it. "Maybe we could hang out sometime...as friends?"

A smile twitched on my lips. I could tell that now the pretense was over, it had taken a great deal of courage to ask that.

I sat down next to him on the sofa. "I'd love that. I really did have more fun last night than I remember ever having before."

"Until we were almost eaten by a dragon, you mean?" he teased, casually bumping my side.

"Actually, you running me back to your home and making pancakes for me was my favorite part," I said, remembering the evening before and how we'd stayed up late, eating pancakes with raspberry jam and chocolate sauce. Then I thought back to how I had felt when I was with him. "I felt safe with you," I whispered.

Milo sighed and looked right into my eyes. "It's a shame your mother doesn't feel the same way... I would have kept you safe, Azia."

I put my hand on his. He was warm, and touching him, even in such an innocent way had me wishing for more. "I know you would have. If things were different, maybe..."

"But you have to marry that buffoon."

I laughed at his choice of words. I had a feeling that Caspian would not like to be called a buffoon. He was one, but that didn't mean he had to like it.

I mulled everything over in my mind. "If only there was some way we could make my parents believe we are in love," I said idly. "Maybe if they could see that, they would change their minds."

"I could think of a way," he said softly. I was keenly aware his hand was still in mine.

He tightened his grip, which forced me to remember the night before when he'd introduced me as his girlfriend. This was all too real for him.

"But it can't be real, remember?" I said, pulling my hand back. "I can't. I just can't. I don't want a boyfriend. I'm sorry." I was playing with his emotions and felt dreadful.

Milo nodded. "I understand. No boyfriend. I already told you I get it. I could fake love you all you need and when the time comes... if you change your mind..."

"I won't," I said, a little too quickly. "Not for a long time anyway. I want to travel first."

"It's fine. I was only teasing you."

He wasn't, and we both knew it.

"Where do we start then?" he said a little too jovially. It broke the tension that had been building between us. Now we were all business. It made things so much easier without worrying about emotions being added to the mix.

Where did we start? How should I know? I knew what love looked like. My parents were like walking Valentine's cards around each other. Songs were written about the love they shared for each other, but how could I replicate it?

Everything they did was so intimate. They didn't stop gazing into each other's eyes for a second, and when they thought no one was looking, they'd often sneak kisses. I couldn't do any of that.

"How about we start by holding hands when my parents are around. That would show them we are in love. It would piss Caspian off to boot."

As though I'd summoned him, the fae walked through the door.

Taking me by surprise, lips pressed against mine. Milo pulled me towards him, wrapping one arm around my waist, the other cradling my face. He tasted of peppermint, and as his warm lips moved against mine, I felt myself falling into him, moving closer without the need of his arm to guide me. My mind screamed at how wrong this was. This was no fake kiss. This was as real as it got, but my body ignored all thoughts.

It was only when the door slammed shut, that Milo pulled back.

"That works too," I whispered, my heart hammering in my chest.

Across from me, Milo said nothing at all.

5TH JANUARY

I spent the night fretting over both Milo and Caspian. Yeah, Caspian certainly wasn't happy which gave me a sense of satisfaction. Promised to me or not, I didn't want him, and I'd been very honest about it from the start. Milo, on the other hand, was turning out to be the bigger problem. He'd kissed me for show, but there was nothing fake about the kiss. Echoes of it had peppered my dreams all night, and I could still almost feel the warmth of his lips on mine and the way my body responded to it. My first kiss, ever! It should have been a moment to cherish in my memory, not something that induced heart-pounding guilt. Although thinking about it had my heart pounding for other reasons too.

The whole thing was a mess. Why did everything have to be so complicated?

It was a relief when my father asked me to go out on a ride with him. At least, I wouldn't be in the castle wondering, which of the two to avoid the most.

After saddling up the horses, we set out into the blistering cold day. Once again, thick white clouds threatened snow.

"Where are we heading, Father?" I asked, cantering out of the castle grounds to the bridge that would take us to the fields.

He galloped a little to catch up. This was something we did often, go for rides together in the warm weather, but today wasn't warm, and I had a feeling this wasn't a casual ride for fun.

"We are heading into Zhore, but first I need to check the base of the mountains." I opened my mouth to ask why when he spoke again.

"I hate superstition, but I cannot deny that the last two incidents involving the dragons have made me nervous."

I cast a side-glance at him. He looked forward, his face set in grim determination, his cheeks already reddening in the blistering cold.

As I breathed out, my breath made its own little clouds. It rarely got cold enough in Draconis to do that. "Do you really believe the dragons will bring about dark times? I don't really see the correlation."

My father shrugged, passing me slightly on his horse. "I don't want to believe it. I consider myself a rational man, but dark magic has ways of getting through. I'm hoping it is merely a human aggravating them that has caused it. That is why we are out today. I've ordered a long fence to be put up along the base of the mountains. It won't keep the dragons out, but it will keep any humans from going in, and hopefully, that will be an end to the problem. The mountain range is thousands of miles around, so I've tasked almost my whole army on it. Let's just hope that our neighbors don't intend to attack, huh?" He laughed mirthlessly.

He meant his words as a joke, but they left unease in my gut as I considered our one true neighbor. On one side of us stood the peaceful kingdom of Badalah. To the south, our kingdom bordered Urbis for a while, but Urbis didn't really count as a kingdom. It was controlled by men in suits and governed all the kingdoms to some extent. Any king or queen could make a law for their own kingdom, but first, that law must get passed by the governors in Urbis before it could be used. To our north and east, rugged coastline stretched for miles bordering the great sea. Badalah would never attack us. Their king, the great Aladdin, and my father had met many times and got on well.

My father picked up the pace once we rode past the pastures and out onto the moors. I raced to keep up with him, but the wind in my face as the first snow began to fall took my breath away. I usually only saw snow on the top of the fire mountains in the deepest part of winter, but every few years or so, a dusting of snow would fall making everything white for a few hours before it thawed and the landscape turned red again. Even the weather, it seemed threatened to prove my father right about dark times coming.

Eventually, we came upon a group of men and women clad in fur coats, working against the weather to erect the fence, which stretched out miles behind them. The few small snowflakes that had begun to fall turned into flurries as my father jumped down from his horse.

"How are things coming?" My father asked what looked to be the man in charge. He was a thickset man with furs wrapped around him tied by a belt that strained.

"It's going to take weeks," the man said gruffly. "If the snow keeps up, it could run into months."

My father glanced up at the sky. At least, the dragons remained hidden from us by the snow-ladened clouds. Pulling my arms around myself to keep out the cold, I listened in to my father's conversation.

"It won't snow for long. It hasn't snowed like this since..."

"Since the dark days," huffed the man. "I know, but I still

maintain that this is a waste of our precious time and resources. With dragons attacking, we need to be in the towns and cities ready to fight, not stuck out here in this cruddy weather building a wall that a dragon could fly over."

My father sighed, moving closer to the man. I noticed that the other workers had now stopped what they were doing and were listening in to what my father had to say.

"I've explained my reasoning, Jacob. I don't believe the dragons are coming down here to hurt us."

"Coulda fooled me," Jacob said, folding his arms around his rotund middle. "I suppose they were breathing fire in the main town to keep us all warm, eh?"

Behind Jacob, some of his crew smirked.

My father held firm. "I understand your frustrations, but I've given you a job, and I expect you to do it. Liking it is optional."

I gave my father a silent cheer as he stood up to Jacob. Jacob, on the other hand, scowled, his face sour.

"I'd rather send all my people up the mountain and kill the bloody lot of them," Jacob responded. "If we do it at once, they won't know what's hit them."

My father shook his head and jumped back on his horse. "I've given you my orders. No one is to go up these mountains until we find out why the dragons are coming down. There will be severe consequences for anyone that disobeys my order."

With that, he turned his horse around and began to walk back towards the road that would take us to Zhore.

"Some of the people don't like the way I'm dealing with things," my father admitted once we'd trotted out of earshot of the fence crew.

"I can understand why he is upset, but he had no right to talk to you like that. Besides, I don't like the thought of anyone killing the dragons. This is all some big mistake. I honestly think someone disturbed them."

My father gave a low chuckle. "You really like the dragons, don't you?"

"I think they are misunderstood," I said, tugging the reins to the right to take us on the path to Zhore. "They've been peaceful for over eighteen years. Creatures don't change habits on a whim, not even dragons."

"I hope you're right, Azia," my father answered slowly. "I really do."

We rode in silence for a mile or so as the snow became heavier around us. "Why are we going to Zhore?" I asked.

"I need to show my face there," he explained. "Ninety percent of being a leader is presence. There is little damage, and those with injuries will make full recoveries, but people are scared. They need a leader to let them know that they will be alright."

That would have comforted me if I knew that he thought things would be all right, but he was flailing along with the rest of us.

It took longer than usual to reach Zhore, owing to the blanket of white snow. Despite the weather, hundreds of people came out to see my father, filling the main square like the audience at a somber music concert. While my father took to a stage to tell everyone about the fence being built, I walked around the square, glancing in the shop windows. I'd not prepared myself for the blistering cold and my fingers hurt.

As all eyes watched my father giving his speech, no one bothered me as I walked the perimeter of the square, checking out the shop windows as I walked, hoping to find one that sold gloves.

At the very back corner, away from the stage, I found a shop that looked like I might be in luck. Tucked away down a small dark alley away from the main square, stood a shop with a sign plainly saying Zhore Wool Shop. If it sold wool, hopefully, it would sell things made from wool too.

I headed into the alley, but when I came to the storefront, I saw something that made my heart seize with fright. There in the shop window stood a spindle.

I'd never seen one in real life before, but I knew exactly what it was. My grandfather had ordered all spindles to be burned when my mother was young. Once my father had become king, he'd ordered spindles to be made illegal. It had been a huge controversy at the time, putting a great many people out of jobs, but the people had forgiven him, knowing it was to keep their beloved queen safe. Well, most of them had. We had to import wool from other kingdoms now, and some of the people didn't like it.

Part of me wanted to run away from the thing, pretend it didn't exist, but my rational mind took over. It was only a spindle, after all. A device for spinning wool. It was not harmful nor dangerous.

Taking a deep breath, I pulled open the door to the shop and walked in. Balls of wool in many colors lined one wall, and throughout the rest of the shop, to my relief were items made from said wool, including a pair of mittens. Picking them up, I headed to the till. Behind the counter, a tall, slim lady watched me warily as I approached. When I placed the mittens on the counter, she broke into a smile. Perfectly straight white teeth filled her mouth, and black-green heavily lidded eyes looked upon me, sending a shiver down my spine. Something about her put me on edge, but I couldn't say what. She was dressed perfectly normally with a purple shawl covering her shoulders, but her eyes bore into mine.

"Is that it, my love?" she asked, her voice brittle and croaky.

"What?"

"The mittens, dear. Is that all you want today?"

"Oh, yes," I said, feeling dazed. I handed over the little bit of cash I happened to have in my pocket and picked the mittens up. That was it. I'd gotten what I'd come for, so now it was time to leave. I'd almost made it to the door when the spindle caught my eye again.

I should have left well alone, but it intrigued me, and I had a strange compulsion to go close to it, to reach out and touch it.

"Is this spindle real?" I asked, turning back to the strange woman.

"Oh, yes, my love. How do you think I come to have so many balls of wool. It's the easiest way to make it."

"But it's illegal," I blurted out. "My grandfather ordered all the spindles to be burned many years ago."

Her expression changed at the mention of my grandfather, but she soon plastered on that white smile again. "Did he? It must have been before I moved here because I don't remember it. Besides. If I burned my spindle, how would I spin my wool? And if I couldn't spin my wool, how would I be able to sell mittens to young ladies such as yourself?"

I shook my shoulders. I didn't want to rob her of her livelihood by telling my father about the spindle. What harm could it do really?

"What harm can it do?" she said almost as if she read my thoughts. "Go and take a closer look. You can see for yourself how harmless it is."

I stepped towards the spindle.

"Go on, touch it."

I jumped. Her voice was right behind me, whispering in my ear. How had she moved across the shop floor so quickly? My mind felt thick with fog, but all I could see was the spindle, and all I could hear were her words.

"Just touch it, my love, and you'll see for yourself that it is nothing to worry your pretty little head over."

Urged on by her words, I held my finger out, ready to bring it down upon the spindle.

"Azia, there you are."

A deep voice made me jump, snapping me out of the fog.

I turned to the door of the shop where my father was waiting. "I've been looking all over for you. What are you doing in here?"

"I was just buying mittens," I said, holding the pair up to show him. My head felt groggy as if I'd only just woken up from a long sleep. I turned back to the woman to thank her for the mittens, but she stood once again back behind the counter, a sour expression on her face. Hurrying out of the shop, I followed my father to where we'd tied up the horses. It was only when we were halfway back that, I realized I'd not pointed the spindle out to my father. Deciding to let it go, I followed my father back to the castle.

When I got home, my mother greeted me at the door. She must have been watching out of the window for our return. She still looked dreadful, but at least, she wasn't in bed any longer.

"I'm sorry I missed you leaving this morning, Azia, darling, but I've had a lovely day with Caspian, and as time is ticking, I really think it's time for you to get to know him."

"He called Remy an idiot," I reminded her. "I don't want to get to know him."

My mother considered this for a second before guiding me back into the drawing room. This time no tray of tea and cookies greeted us. I guess it was so close to dinnertime that she hadn't bothered.

"I spoke to him about that," she said, closing the door behind her. "He says that you misheard him."

"Dragon dung!"

"Azia, please. Keep your voice down and mind your language," she admonished. "That's no way for a princess to talk."

I sat down on the sofa, and she took a seat beside me. "Maybe not, but I heard him perfectly." I knew I had. My mother took my hand in hers, reminding me how Milo had held my hand only yesterday before kissing me on this very sofa.

"As you say," my mother said, taking me away from the thought. "But he's spent a lot of time with Remy today. He even let him touch his sword, and you know how much Remy likes swords."

"He spent time with Remy?" I thought back to the time I'd seen him by the pasture watching Remy and I play sword fighting. He'd looked upon Remy with such disdain. He'd looked at me the same way. As though we were dragon crap on his shoe. Why did he want to marry me so much and why spend time with Remy? I hated to think of my brother playing with that jerk.

"Is Remy alright?" I hardly dared ask.

My mother tutted and brought up her hand. "Don't be silly, Azia. Of course, he's all right. I was watching them the whole time. He only let him touch the hilt of the sword, not the sharp end."

I wasn't thinking about the sword. Caspian used magic that messed with people's minds. Remy was defenseless against him.

"Now, what do you say about you two spending the day together tomorrow?" she asked lightly. "You could do something fun."

Yeah, like garrotte the ass with cheese wire. That would be fun.

"I kissed Milo last night," I stated in the hope this might sway her.

She pursed her lips and narrowed her eyes. The faint hint of laughter lines appeared in her tired face. "I heard," she said brusquely. "You will have to stop seeing him, Azia. It's the only way. Give Caspian a chance, he really has been a dream today, and he's awfully beautiful."

She left me no choice in the matter. What might have seemed like a simple request was not a request at all. It was an order. I nodded.

"Yes, Ma'am." It probably wouldn't be too bad as long as neither of us killed the other. Or if I killed him first. I could pass it off as an accident.

"I'll do as you ask, but that doesn't mean I will come back from our date wanting to marry him."

My mother brought me into a hug. "The way things are going, you may have to whether you like it or not. Now, go along and tell Milo it's over between the two of you. The longer you draw it out, the harder it will be for all involved, and I don't want a mopey guard protecting the castle at a time like this. The quicker he can get over you, the better."

I nodded my head, too depressed to answer, but when I left the drawing room it wasn't Milo I went to see, it was Remy. I needed to know he was all right after his day with the faery. Mother might have not seen anything, but that meant nothing when Caspian was involved. It didn't take me long to find him. He spent a lot of his time in the library. He could barely talk, but he knew how to read. He enjoyed books more than anything in the world. He loved adventure books the most, stories of swashbucklers and pirates. I think it let him escape from who he really was. He could pretend to be free of his own mind and body.

The library was also my favorite room in the house. Bookshelf after bookshelf filled with every book imaginable, from books on the history of Draconis to adventure books that Remy liked to read. I found him laid out on the library floor, a number of books open next to him. When he saw me, a grin crept onto his face.

"Aza, pira." He ran over to me and took one of my hands into his huge bear paws. Picking up the book he'd been reading, he thrust it at me, eager to share today's adventure.

"Pirates, arrgh," I said, making him giggle.

If only all my relationships were as easy as the one I had with my younger brother. He never asked me for anything beyond reading to him, and he always made time for me.

"Arrgh," he replied, giggling and thrusting a make-believe sword at me.

I jumped back, my hands in the air, which only brought about more giggles.

He seemed ok. Maybe the day with the faery hadn't upset him, after all, and I was worrying about nothing.

"It's nearly time for dinner," I said, picking up some of the books he'd casually dropped all over the floor. "Can you help me put the books back on the shelves?"

He nodded eagerly, and between us, we picked up all the books he'd gotten out and placed them back in their places.

Hollis and Ash were already waiting at the dinner table as Remy and I walked in. Seconds later, my mother followed, hand in hand with my father.

Thankfully, Casplan was nowhere to be seen.

"Azia and Milo sitting in a tree," Ash started, and beside him, Hollis began to laugh as though this was the funniest thing he'd ever heard. Then, of course, Remy started laughing because his brothers were, even though he didn't know why.

"Aren't you a bit old for that?" I accused, throwing him shade across the table.

"Stop it, the pair of you," my mother admonished. "I'm tired enough as it is." She held her hand to her head as my father pulled the chair out for her.

"K.I.S.S.I.N.G.," Hollis added under his breath. It was a good thing my parents adopted me; otherwise, one of these morons would one day be running the kingdom.

After suffering through dinner, I decided to head back to my room, needing to spend some time to think things through. Everything had suddenly turned so chaotic. I knew that transitioning from a child to an adult was never easy, but this was ridiculous. One week on from my eighteenth birthday and the entire kingdom had gone insane, not to mention my parents. If I'd have known turning eighteen would make everything so weird, I'd have stayed seventeen forever and just spent my days out in the pasture, practicing my sword fighting. My heart fell a little at the thought of it. I'd not been out with my sword in over two weeks. Practicing my sword fighting was the only time when I felt free. With a rush of excitement, I increased my steps, back to my room to pick up my sword. It was only when I entered my corridor that I remembered that Caspian had magicked it away the night he came into my room.

"Dragon balls!" I muttered under my breath.

"On toast?" a voice asked. Milo stood there in his position outside my room. This was his corridor to guard, so it wasn't infeasible for him to be there. The last time I'd seen him, we'd shared the most amazing kiss, and now that he stood in front of me, the nerves began to creep in.

"What?" I asked.

"It's a saying my father used to say. He got it from the dwarves. Dragon balls on toast. It was one of the few he picked up that I can repeat in front of a princess." He gave me a lazy grin

My lip quirked up at the edge, but his humor was not what I needed. I needed to vent my frustration, and fighting - even with an invisible foe was the only way I knew how.

"Are you ok?" he asked, catching my expression. I guess my smile didn't quite extend to my eyes.

"I was going to go and practice my sword skills, but I've er...lost my sword."

A look of comprehension dawned on his face. "Ah, so that's why you've not been out practicing so much lately."

My cheeks colored and I stared at the floor so as to not accidentally look him in the eyes. "Do you watch me a lot out there?"

"I don't make a habit of it, but sometimes I see you out of that window on the end of the corridor there." He pointed to the small round window.

"I thought I was well-hidden around the back of the castle. My parents wouldn't like it if they knew what I was doing, my mother especially."

He stood so close to me that I could barely breathe. The memory of the kiss fluttered into my mind, taking root there and making me want to run away. If only I hadn't enjoyed it as much as I had.

He nodded. "I think you are fine. I doubt any other windows show that exact spot, and your mother rarely comes up here. I've only ever seen her on this corridor once in the seven months I've worked here, and that was when Remy was sick."

"Well, then, I should..."

I pointed to my door. This was ridiculous. He was my guard. Actually, he wasn't even that. He was just one of a number of guards assigned to this particular corridor. I had no reason to feel shy around him...because that's exactly how I felt. Before the kiss, I was so sure I didn't want a boyfriend or husband. Even now, the day after the kiss, I was still sure, but something was different. Before the kiss, this whole thing was a fun game. Now it had turned serious, and like a freight train with broken breaks, I didn't know how to stop it.

He nodded slowly and gave me a look. The look someone gives you when they are being let down. A half-smile didn't quite reach his eyes. It pained me, but what could I do? He shouldn't have kissed me in the first place...and he shouldn't have been so damn good at it.

I closed my bedroom door behind me and breathed out a sigh of relief. I'd not even noticed I was holding my breath. When I'd let my heart rate drop to an acceptable level, I walked over to the window. Outside in the distance, the workers erecting the fence were still going at it. It was probably a different crew. My father said they'd be working day and night until the whole mountain range was fenced in. It seemed such a ludicrous proposition. The Fire Mountains took up the whole northeast of Draconis before they tapered off into the sea. They would need hundreds, if not thousands of miles of fencing. All to stop anyone deciding to climb up them to steal an egg.

I lay back in frustration, wondering what else I could do to calm my nerves. Jumping up, I decided to go for a run.

Outside, the snow was coming down thickly, laying a blanket of fine white powder. Not the best weather to run in, but it was either that or go stir crazy. Breaking into a jog, I lapped the castle three times, before stopping in the hidden space I usually practiced in. An area at the back of the castle that no one had any reason to venture to but me. Glancing up at the round window, on the second floor, I half expected Milo to be watching me from it, but there was no one there.

Bending over to catch my breath, I heard the damp crunch of footsteps on snow. Looking up, I saw Milo standing before me as though thinking about him had made him appear. He was holding the ruby sword. My breath caught at the sight of it.

He held it out to me, the sharp end in his gloved hand.

I looked at him, ignoring the excitement in the pit of my belly. If this was a gift of love, I could never accept it, but there was no expression on his face at all.

Taking the sword from his hand, I once again felt the power in the Dwarves' metal as though the sword and I connected somehow.

"Thank you," I whispered.

"I can only let you take this sword on one condition," he said solemnly. "You are an amazing swordsperson. I've watched you practice, but you lack training. Thanks to your father, I've been trained among the best. Let me teach you. Let me refine your talent and make you the swordswoman I know you can be."

Excitement flooded through me at the thought of it.

"Thank you," I whispered.

I doubted my parents would take too kindly to him training me, and if we got caught, he would surely lose his job. He must have thought the same thing because he took my hand and led me to the wall that surrounded the castle. At the back, a small door led to a wooded area. Together we stole through the door and entered the woods.

I'd never been in these woods before. I had never had reason to, so I let Milo lead me to wherever he wanted me to go. He stopped at an open area where the trees thinned out a little, letting the snow fall lightly through. Inside, a circle was drawn into the snow.

"This is our training area," he said, pointing to the circle. "I came here earlier and set it up."

I raised my eyebrows.

"I knew you'd come," he said with a grin, making my stomach squirm.

Next to the circle on a rock, sat two sets of protective clothes made of leather and metal.

"Will we be safe in here?" I asked. My fear was not for wolves or other creatures, but of a member of the castle staff strolling through and accidentally coming upon us. My mother would pitch a fit if she knew where I was...and with whom.

"No one comes here," he said, throwing one of the protective breastplates at me. "Put that on."

Pulling it over my head, I let it drop, hanging from my shoulders. It weighed me down. This would hamper my movements.

"Is this necessary?" I asked, pulling the buckles tight.

"I'm not going to take it easy on you, and I don't expect you to take it easy on me. I'm not teaching you to dance, I'm teaching you to protect yourself, to kill if necessary. That sword I've given you will slice a limb off as easily as it would slice a tomato. Seeing as I'm partial to all my limbs, I'd say that this is entirely necessary."

His words sent a shiver of nerves running through me, followed by a thrill of excitement. I'd been wanting this from the very first time I'd been allowed to watch my father's men training. The training arena stood within the castle grounds, and after that first time, I'd steal into it and watch them. It was there that I developed my love of fighting. I'd been practicing ever since, first with sticks as pretend swords, and then with the stolen sword from the armory.

Once our protective suits covered us, I picked my sword back up and waited for Milo.

"You're standing wrong," he said, walking toward me. I let him position my arms and legs, trying to ignore the thrill of electricity running up my legs as he clasped each ankle in turn and moved them so they were about a foot apart.

He worked his way up, moving my body until he was satisfied.

"This is the strongest position. One foot slightly in front

of the other, your body slightly twisted. You want to give your opponent the least amount of space to stab you. Hold your sword out in front of you, then swipe it to the side. That is your fighting space. You do not, under any circumstances, want your opponent in that space. I am going to attack you now. Don't worry, the armor will protect you. Your job is not to kill me; it is only to defend that space. I don't want to be able to get anywhere near you. Ok?"

I nodded. It sounded easy. Stop him getting close to me. I'd been doing the exact same thing metaphorically with no luck, but hopefully, I'd do better with the physical stuff. He bowed down, and I followed suit before readying myself in the stance he showed me.

"Go!" he shouted out.

My hand stiffened around my sword. I was ready.

Three seconds later, my sword was on the ground beside me and Milo's lips pecked my own, taking my breath away.

"What was that?" I asked him.

"I stole a kiss," he grinned. "Any other opponent would skewer your heart."

I doubted anyone would be able to find my heart, as it seemed to be doing a rumba around my chest.

Picking up the sword, I readied myself again, gritting my teeth in anticipation.

"Go!" I shouted. He ran toward me and this time I dodged. He missed, but then from behind, he once again swiped my sword from my hand. When I turned, he stole another kiss.

Trying to keep the amused smile from my face and hide the fact that my whole body was trembling, thanks to his kisses, I picked my sword up once again.

"That wasn't fair. You cheated."

"I'm trying to kill you, remember?" he said, dancing around me. "I'm your enemy. Do you think I care if you think I cheated? I am alive, and you are dead."

"You really are going to kill me at this rate," I huffed, taking up the stance again. We practiced for hours, taking it in turns to "kill" one another. By the time our only light was starlight, he'd given me one hundred and thirty-three kisses. I'd not managed to strike him once.

"Let's call it a night," Milo said. "It's dark, and I have to get home." He placed his sword on the stone to pull his armor off, and that's when I saw my chance. Swiping his feet from under him, I elbowed him in the side so he toppled over. Without giving him time to recover, I dropped on top of him, pinning him to the ground below, my legs straddling his stomach. The tip of my sword rested right over the metal plate covering his heart."

"I killed you," I whispered.

"You cheated," he responded. "I'd already put my sword down."

"I'm your enemy out for the kill," I said, echoing his own words from earlier. "Do you think I care that I cheated?" I lowered my sword to his side and took my own victory kiss. This time it was not just a peck on the lips.

6TH JANUARY

"Let's go for a walk, shall we?" The fae held out his hand for me after breakfast.

I looked toward my mother, who yawned, then when she caught me looking, nodded her head.

"Fine," I capitulated. There was no way I was holding the guy's hand, though. He could walk next to me...or behind me...or off a cliff. Whatever.

"Interesting weather we are having," Caspian mused as we stepped out into the snow. "I was under the impression it barely snows in Draconis, but it's worse than a Forge winter."

"Hmm," I sighed non-committedly. Who cared what the weather in The Forge was like. "Why don't you head back there?"

I picked up my pace as we headed across the bridge out onto the pastures.

"You've not liked me from the start, but there's no reason not to," he began.

I cut him off. "Really? Because I can think of at least three reasons off the top of my head, and I'm sure if I thought a bit longer, I could come up with more."

"Please stop. I don't like playing games."

I turned to face him, annoyance filling me. He was beautiful without the sneer he usually wore, which put me off guard, but I was too angry to let a bit of gorgeousness get in the way. "Who's playing games? I've been very honest from the start with you. That's not game-playing."

I brought my hands up to my hips and gave him my best, prove me wrong look. Unfortunately, to him, the challenge was a red flag to a bull, and he was nothing if not bull-headed.

"The romance with your guard is fabricated, and that feels a lot like game-playing to me," he growled, bringing his face close to mine. His disdain for me was overwhelming, though I could also see desire in his eyes. I don't know which annoyed me more. "If I wanted to be messed around by women, I could have stayed in The Forge."

I swayed slightly on my heels and resisted the urge to kick him. "How did you... never mind. It doesn't matter. If you are somehow reading my mind, you'll see that I don't want to marry you." He'd also see that my fake romance with Milo was becoming more real by the day and the whirl of emotions that went along with that. It wasn't Caspian I saw when I closed my eyes at night. It was Milo. That was a problem to deal with later. Right now, dealing with Caspian was taking up all of my energy.

He narrowed his eyes. "I don't need to read your mind to know that. You've made it very clear. I also don't need to be a mind reader to know about you and Milo. When I saw you kissing him the other night, you seemed genuinely shocked. If you two were dating, why would you be so shocked to be kissed by him? It was only a hunch up until now, but you've confirmed it. I can't read minds, by the way. Manipulate them a little, but not read them. Very few fae can, but I can read clues. I like to watch people."

He smiled languidly as he caught me out in my lie. Dragon shit! I gritted my teeth and sucked in a deep breath, which froze in my lungs, causing me to cough.

The faery waited for me to stop coughing before continuing to speak. "Look, I know we've gotten off on the wrong foot, and I also know that it's mostly my fault."

"Mostly?" I questioned raising an eyebrow, tears running down my face from the coughing. I wiped my eyes on the back of my sleeve, hoping he didn't think the tears were something to do with him.

"Ok," he relented, putting his hands in the air. "It's all my fault. I've been insensitive and rude, and I've made mistakes. I came here because your father asked me to. He thought that he owed me for something I did for him a long time ago. That's why he offered you to me."

"You make it sound like I'm a pig in a meat market," I barked, narrowing my eyes at him.

"Hardly, but your father does owe me, and he thought I'd make a good husband for you."

Ignoring the squeezing sensation in my stomach, I asked him through gritted teeth why my father owed him.

He beckoned me onwards, away from the castle. "We were friends many years ago, and back then, he asked me for magical help to get through the enchanted brambles that surrounded the castle."

I turned to him. "That's not what I was told. The curse had ended anyway. That's why he was able to get through the brambles when so many others had failed before him. He told me that cutting through them was easier than he'd been led to believe."

The fae nodded thoughtfully. "Maybe that's true, but why? What was it that ended that curse if not me? Only a couple of weeks before your father attempted it, someone died trying the exact same thing. Many people lost their lives in the attempt to save your mother. Your father found it difficult, but as you say, the brambles were dying. What was it that changed? That curse was never meant to be a hundred-year curse. It was meant to last forever, a testament to Derillen's power."

"Derillen?" I'd never heard the name before. "Who is Derillen?"

The fae kept his eyes ahead, looking into the distance as he spoke. "It seems I've spoken out of term. If you do not know that name, it is not my place to enlighten you."

Anger coursed through me. Why was it that every time I spoke to this man, I wanted to stick a sword through his ribs? I thought back to the dragon sword carefully hidden in my room and wished I'd had the forethought to bring it with me.

"Why won't you tell me?"

"It is not my place to," he said. "There is no point in getting angry with me. It is not I that has spent your whole life keeping secrets from you. Perhaps you should ask your parents."

I stalked off ahead in the snow. New snow dropped constantly, transforming the landscape into a winter wonderland. I watched my breath in the frigid air, transforming me almost into the fire-and-smoke-breathing dragons everyone feared so much.

"Let's talk about something else," Caspian said, catching up. "We are to be married soon, and I would like to find some common ground with you."

I huffed. "I can't think of a single thing the pair of us have in common." I trudged ahead of him again, but something stopped me. As if a net had been thrown over me, I felt myself being pulled back, my feet making tracks in the snow.

When I ended up back next to him, he waved his hand and the invisible ropes pulling me disappeared.

I glared at him, ready to give him the tongue-lashing he deserved, but he spoke first.

"Actually, I think we have more in common than you know."

"Give me one example," I fumed, folding my arms across my chest.

He cocked his head thoughtfully before bringing his hand back up.

I felt the ropes around me again, but this time they crushed my arms to my chest and locked my legs together. Falling into the snow, I fought against the invisible bonds that had taken hold. Beside me, Caspian held out his hand, his fingers splayed, his mouth silently working his magic. If I had my sword, the dwarf magic in the metal would cut through the strands of magic like butter, but I didn't. I was defenseless.

"What are you doing?" I screamed, letting snow enter my mouth. Swallowing back the freezing water, I fought against my magical chains as the fae watched on with interest.

"I'm not trying to hurt you, but the more you move, the more painful it will be. Hold still and fight back properly."

Fight back properly? When I was free of his magic, I was going to knock his block off.

I squirmed against my binds as they cut into my clothes and bit into my skin. As soon as I became still, the pain subsided, and the ropes or chains loosened a little. More squirming and they bit down again.

"Let me go," I hissed through chattering teeth as the snow began to melt into my trousers, soaking me to the skin.

"Make me," he answered back, his teeth gleaming from the wide smile he gave me.

They would be the first to go, I mused, as I contemplated punching him right in his beautiful mouth.

"You aren't even trying," Caspian goaded, tapping his toe

in the soft snow as he waved his hands around to keep the magic flowing.

"What exactly do you want me to do?" I hissed through chattering teeth.

He bent down until his face was close to mine. Not close enough for me to head-butt him, but close enough to see how much he was enjoying this. "I've seen something in you that excites me, but it looks like I'm going to be let down. I'm very rarely wrong, but it has been known to happen."

"What are you talking about?" I screeched. I was going to get hypothermia if I wasn't careful. Or if he wasn't.

"Magic, Azia. I'm talking about magic. I can feel it in you, but I wonder if you can feel it yourself." He pulled back his hand, and I found myself rising into the air. When I was about six feet from the ground, he began to spin me around.

The world tumbled about me as I spun in the air.

"Stop it," I yelled as darkness appeared at the edge of my consciousness, threatening to make me black out.

"Make me," he yelled back.

Anger surged through me like never before. Fury raged, warming my belly. Make him? I was going to kill him, the first chance I got, my mother and my marriage be damned.

The warmth became energy, which became something else entirely. In front of me, the world toppled end over end, the mountains, becoming Caspian and then going back to the mountains again. While inside, I burned with sizzling energy.

With a primordial scream, I let the energy go before it burned through me. With a bump, the soft snow flew up beneath me, and I landed on the ground. With shaky legs, I stood. It took all my energy not to fall over again, thanks to the dizziness that engulfed me.

"I will murder you!" I muttered, holding a shaky finger

out to Caspian's face. My feet wobbled, wanting to topple beneath me, and it took everything I had not to let them.

The fae had the gall to laugh.

"I wasn't wrong. I didn't think I was. You are magic."

His words pierced the fog in my brain.

"What?"

"You have magic in you. I didn't let you go. You fought against my magic. Now, I don't like to brag, but I'm pretty powerful. Not the most powerful in all the kingdoms, but it would take a lot of magic to be able to cut through those bonds that held you. You did that, my dear, not I."

"I'm not magic," I whispered, faltering.

"How do you know?" he asked, brushing my hair back over my ears. "You don't have the pointed ears, so you are not fae, but I suspect your magic is powerful. Maybe even more so than mine. You were adopted, so you don't know your birth parents. How do you know that you are even human?"

"Of course, I'm human!" I shouted at him, then proceeded to throw up all over his shoes.

It took a good few minutes of sitting in the snow before my head stopped spinning entirely. While I sat with my head in my hands, my ass getting soaked by the wet snow, Caspian performed spell after spell over his puke-covered shoes, trying to make them clean again. Eventually, he waved his hand over them and made them disappear, before conjuring a pair of boots from thin air.

When he'd put them on, he waved his hand at me. Below me, a picnic blanket appeared, and a warmth came over me, drying my clothes out immediately. I went from shivering and cold to warm and cozy in a second. He sat beside me and conjured up a large umbrella to stop the snow falling upon us. When he'd done that, he performed his last piece of magic and set out a spread of food for us.

Now that I'd calmed down and my head no longer spun, I

decided to let him live. At least, until we ate. I'd consider it again once the food was gone.

He poured me a glass of wine and handed it over.

"A celebration for your first performance of magic. The fae always celebrate a child's first act of magic. Usually, it is when they are young, three or four perhaps. But I think that this merits a celebration even if you are not fae."

"I am human," I reiterated, taking a sip of the wine. The sweet nectar ran down my throat, warming me from the inside out.

The fae shrugged. "Maybe, maybe not, but how do you know?"

He'd already asked me that. It was obvious I was a human. What else could I be? "Because I look human. I feel human, and as you pointed out, I don't have any markings of being a fae. Apart from my title of princess, I'm as ordinary as it gets."

The fae shook his head. "That isn't true. I knew you were far from ordinary from the first moment I saw you. Magic attracts magic, and I felt a strong attraction to you that had nothing to do with sexual attraction. It was more than that, something magnetic. Now I'm not saying that I don't feel sexual attraction to you too. I do, but this is most definitely something different."

I blushed at his words. He was so forthcoming. I chose, however, to skip over the sexual attraction part and move back to the magic part of the conversation. "I only have it on your word that I am magic. I don't feel magic. You could have stopped your own magic, and I would have fallen into the snow exactly the same."

"True," he said, picking up a sandwich, "But I didn't. You did it all by yourself. Only someone of greater power than mine would have been able to do that."

I shook my head. "Surely, if I was magic, I would have noticed before now?"

"Not necessarily. Your power is greater than even I expected when I first met you. When you cut those bonds spinning you, I felt the heat in your magic. If I wasn't as strong as I was, it would have sent me flying. It might be worth talking to your parents. There are obviously things they haven't told you. I don't even know all the answers myself. When you were adopted, there was an announcement in the papers. It was only a matter of weeks after they married. They hadn't even gone on honeymoon yet. I asked your father once why they had adopted you so soon. They were still very young, only eighteen themselves. They had their whole life ahead of them. Your father wouldn't say more than the newspapers told me. Then, when they did go on honeymoon, your mother fell pregnant with your eldest brother. They became a family very quickly. I wonder if that had something to do with the questions you ask."

I contemplated his words. Like any other orphan, I'd thought about my birth parents from time to time, wondered who they were. I'd been told very little, though my mother had been honest with me from the start about it. At least, I thought she had been until today.

The reason I'd never probed further about my birth parents was that I simply didn't want to know. I was the princess of Draconis, the heir to the throne. How could I have come from better than that? I couldn't. I had two loving parents, three brothers and I lived a good life. I had fine clothes, I traveled a lot, and the pain of being given up when I was a baby? Well, I'd buried that deep long ago.

"If I'm magic, why can't I do anything?" I challenged. I waved my hand out in the same manner that he had as if to prove my point, and nothing happened.

"Magic is not just something people can automatically do.

It is a learned skill even by those who possess it. You have to learn to channel it. Didn't you feel it when you broke my bonds?"

I thought back to the warmth in my belly. I had felt something. Something I'd mistaken as anger.

"Here," he said, throwing me an apple. "Turn this into an orange."

I looked at the apple. It looked like any other apple, with shiny red skin. I could no more have turned it into an orange than I could have turned it into a horse.

"No."

"Look at it and envision the shape of it becoming more spherical. Imagine the color changing. Imagine a citrusy smell. Imagine holding an orange in your hand. And when you can see the orange in your mind's eye, do whatever it was that you did back there when you saved yourself from my clutches."

"I imagined stabbing you through the heart with my sword," I answered.

The fae gave a big belly laugh. "If you need to do that to make your magic work, then do it. Once you've mastered it, it will come a lot easier to you."

He pointed back to the apple in my hand. I did as he instructed. Imagining an orange was easy; what I struggled with was bringing all the energy back to my core. Anger at Caspian hurting me had set me off, but now I was no longer angry. Curious, unbelieving and slightly annoyed perhaps, but no emotion big enough to cause the same reaction as last time.

I pulled everything I had into myself. Closing my eyes, I could hear Caspian's words of encouragement. I no longer wanted to kill him, but I remembered how I felt when I did. The energy began to build, and this time, I let it, keeping it churning in my stomach. When I could take it no longer, I channeled it down my arm to the fruit. A bang, followed by something wet splattering my face caused me to open my eyes.

Caspian was covered in mashed up bits of apple, as was I. A black scorch mark was all that was left of the apple in my hand.

"Maybe you need a little more practice," Caspian said and began to laugh again. This time I joined in. "That's it for today. Learning magic is exhausting work, and you need to rest."

He wasn't wrong. My entire body ached with the effort I'd put in. He pulled me up by my hand and magicked the picnic, the umbrella, and the wine away. The snow that had been drifting around us, once again, began to fall on our heads.

"Do you want to go back to the castle or do you want to go on that walk we had planned?"

I glanced over his shoulder. The castle was not far behind him. We'd barely made it to the pasture where we first met. I surprised myself by answering that I did want to walk. Snow was so uncommon here, and now that I was warmed by both Caspian's magic and the wine, I found I wasn't ready to go back to the castle yet. Exhaustion aside, I wanted to see what else I could do. Exploding an apple was one thing, but it had no practical use.

"I told you we had something in common," Caspian said, taking hold of my hand. This time I let him.

"You and I are one of a kind."

"You said that I wasn't fae." I flicked my hair behind my ear to show him my perfectly normal-looking ears. "Remember?"

"Maybe, but you are a person of magic. It's up to you to decide if you want to find out exactly what it is you are. Humans don't have the ability to perform magic. If you ever see a human doing that, if you check his family tree, you'll find something in there. Maybe you are a witch."

"A witch?" A shiver passed through me. Witches had a bad reputation, although there were some known to be good. They used the magic of the earth in their spells. I didn't feel like I was pulling magic from the earth. Whatever my magic was, it came directly from me.

We walked lazily across the snow-covered fields, and for the first time since meeting him, I felt comfortable in his presence. We walked a couple of miles until we were at the base of the Fire Mountains, close to where I'd been with my father. The fence stretched as far as the eye could see in both directions, disappearing into the white of the snow.

Now that I could feel the magic, and understand what it was, I was eager to use it more. "I want to do more magic. I want to learn to do more than change fruit."

"Aren't you tired," he asked, but I could see the amusement in his eyes.

"Yes," I admitted, "but I want to keep going."

"Ok," he capitulated. "What is it you want to do? Make me fall in love with you, maybe?"

I pulled a face, I was sure was not attractive.

"You can't conjure love, no matter how much you'd like to," he added after taking a look at my face.

"That's good to know. I wasn't sure if I'd be able to hold myself back otherwise." I replied.

He gripped my hand tightly before letting it go. "Oh, I do enjoy a spot of sarcasm. What is it you want to learn then?"

I wanted to learn to fight. If I could learn with magic, the same I could learn with a sword, I'd be an invaluable member of my father's army whether he liked it or not. I didn't just want to learn, I wanted to be the best.

"Teach me magical combat."

Caspian sighed, not as excited about the idea as I was.

"You could have asked for anything. How to conjure money, jewels...anything."

"I have all the money and jewels I want. I'm a princess," I said, holding my hands up and waving them down myself. "Jewels hold no interest for me. Knowing how to defend myself in times of trouble. That's what I want to know."

"Defense?" He sighed again. "I suppose teaching you how to defend yourself is not the worst thing I could teach you. Fine, we'll have a magical duel. Whatever you do, do not use your magic to kill. You are stronger than me, and I don't want any accidents."

"You're good. I'm not feeling as murderous as I was a couple of hours ago."

"How reassuring. Let's aim to mark the other's skin with paint. That way, no one will get hurt, and a winner will be clear. Pick a color."

I thought back to the ruby sword. "Red."

He nodded. "I'll be purple. Stand over there and face me. When I say go, I want you to conjure little balls of red paint and fling them at me." He waved his hand, and a clock appeared from nowhere and hung in thin air. "When the clock counts down to zero, time is up. I've set it for ten minutes. The winner is the one least covered in paint. Do you understand?"

I nodded and readied myself, getting into the stance that Milo had taught me the night before. I might not have been fighting with swords, but I was most definitely fighting, and I planned to win.

"I'll give you a few seconds start, to get to grips with everything, but once you take your first shot, it's every man for himself."

He'd barely finished the sentence when an explosion of color hit his chest. Red bloomed, looking like a knife wound. With a grin, he pulled back his hand and launched his own paint. Pretty soon we were running around, launching paint at each other, giggling like schoolchildren. The snow resembled an abstract painting, but I was having too much fun to care. I screamed loudly, laughing as each blast of purple hit me. It was hard to tell who was the most covered in paint. Battlefield fatalities were less bloodied than him, and although I knew his blood was nothing but harmless paint, it didn't make the effect any less horrific. At least, the paint on me was purple and couldn't be mistaken for blood. If anyone came upon us, they wouldn't know what to think. Not that I was worried, the weather was taking a turn for the worse, and the snow fell more thickly. I was about to declare a tie when Caspian volleyed a number of purple globs of paint at me. I screamed again and readied myself to give back as good as I got, when the sky lit up a deep red, coloring the falling snow. Seconds later, a deep roar filled my ears. Caspian ran towards me and grabbed my hand just as the dragon appeared through the clouds. It's giant wings displaced the snow as it opened its mouth to roar again. The smell of burning sulfur filled the air as we ran, the dragon flying behind us.

"Do something," I screamed as another dragon appeared in front of us, blocking our path. The base of the mountains was to our left, which meant the castle was somewhere in front of us, but we'd walked so far, and it was impossible to see through the falling snow. There was nowhere to run to and nowhere to hide.

A blast of fire heated my side as we tried dodging the dragon in front of us. Above us, the snow stopped ominously. I didn't need to look skywards to know it was because yet another dragon was above us, blocking it.

"I can't," Caspian yelled back. "Dragon hide is thick. No magic can pass through it. If they see us fighting back, they'll barbecue us for sure."

But what else was there to do? We were surrounded by them. It was fight or die, and I wasn't ready to die yet. Pulling in the magical energy was easier this time. I had fear coursing through me, which was enough emotion to fuel the magic. So far, my magic had only exploded apples and conjured paint, so this time I'd have to dig deep. Neither of those things would save us from a pack of dragons. I wished for my sword. That would be the most useful, but no amount of wishing or trying to conjure it worked. The magical energy burned as it swirled around inside me, getting hotter and hotter with each passing second. It looked like I was going to fight fire with fire.

I pointed upwards, and a jet of fire rose into the sky, like a beacon, lighting up the snow and showing me just how serious our problem was. There weren't just three or four dragons. There were hundreds of them. The flames rose higher, but then something astonishing happened.

The dragons on the ground lowered themselves so their bellies touched the snow and the ones in the air came in to land, making the earth move every time one of them landed. Pretty soon, we were surrounded by dragons. When my magic finally gave up, my senses kicked in. We were in the dead center of hundreds of dragons, any one of which could kill us in a second.

My mind was in fight or flight mode, but my feet wouldn't move, tethered to the ground, not by magic, but by fear.

Caspian stood next to me, unmoving.

"What is happening?" I whispered

"I don't know. I've never seen anything like this before." The dragons nearest to us lowered their heads, and Caspian clasped my hand. We began to walk slowly through them, neither of us daring to run in case it spooked them. As we passed by, more of them lowered their heads to the snow.

They weren't sick. Their eyes were open and followed us as we passed, but none of them made a move to hurt us. The ones behind us took to the skies, harmlessly flying upwards and the ones in front continued to bow. It was only when we had the castle in sight, and the dragons were long behind us that we began to run, stopping only when we were at the very edge of the pasture.

My nerves were wrecked, and it wasn't helping that Caspian was still covered in red paint and melting snow.

He was a picture of water and blood.

He waved his hand, and the pair of us cleaned up instantly.

"Thank you," I wheezed, not knowing what else to say. "Did you use magic on those dragons?"

He shook his head. "I told you, dragon-hide is impenetrable by magic. The only magic I saw was yours. What did you do?"

I shrugged my shoulders, aware that I was still shaking. "I didn't do anything either. I shot a flame up into the air."

"Well, that flame got those dragons to bow down to you. I've never seen that before. It's not natural for dragons to act that way. You need to speak to your parents about where you came from. You are more powerful than even I first thought. Not even the most powerful mages can control dragons, but, sweetheart...looks like you just did."

He held out his hand to me, but I couldn't take it. I'd enjoyed the day. Well, up until the point a hundred dragons swooped in, but I still didn't want to marry him. Enjoying a day out was one thing. Forgiveness of the things he'd said and done, another, but the feelings that were growing for Milo were something else. I couldn't walk into the castle hand in hand with Caspian in case Milo saw. I'd not given any promises to anyone, but I had a feeling I was giving my heart to Milo.

"I can't. I'm sorry."

His face twisted into a sneer. "I hoped you'd changed your mind. We are getting married as per your father's decree whether you want to or not. I just hoped you would actually want to."

He stalked on ahead, making me run to catch up.

We were in the entrance of the castle before I caught up to him. I needed to thank him for such a nice day and for telling me something about myself that I hadn't even known. Guilt squeezed my heart, and I knew sorry wasn't enough, but I wanted to say it to him anyway. My mother never gave me the chance. She must have heard the door, and she came to greet us before I had chance to apologize.

"Did you have a nice day, you two?" she beamed.

Before I had the chance to speak, Caspian answered for me.

“There is no reason that Azia cannot marry me now. While we were out walking today, she told me that her romance with Milo was fake. The pair of them made it all up to fool you.”

I glared at him with murder in my eyes. How could he do this? Just as I was beginning to like him.

7TH JANUARY

Overnight, the snow had softened, and the sky was clear when I woke up. I'd spent half the night angry at Caspian and the other half waiting for Milo to arrive. He'd not worked the day before, nor had he done a night shift. Therefore, he would be working today. I'd not mentioned anything to my parents about what happened with Caspian the day before. Only he knew about my magic, and only he knew about the dragons. I should have told my parents, at least, that part. My father should know, but I'd gone straight to my room and skipped dinner. After a couple of hours trying to do magic again, I'd finally given up and fallen asleep. I would tell my father about the dragons soon, but it was Milo I wanted to tell first. I wanted to show him my magic too.

The clock hands moved excruciatingly slowly as I waited for them to tick down to nine am when his shift usually started. The fear of him having been fired because of what the fae had told my mother rendered me almost immobile, but at five minutes to nine, I caught him walking past my room to start his shift. I pulled him into my room and closed the door behind me, locking it in case Dahlia or anyone else came to find me.

He kissed me, pulling me into his arms and the anxiety I'd been feeling all night melted away.

"I don't want a boyfriend," I murmured, but it was hard to really push the point home when I followed it up with another kiss.

"Are you ok?" he asked, pulling back, a quizzical expression on his face.

"Yes," I lied. "Why shouldn't I be?"

He glanced around the room. "I can smell burning. Was there a fire?"

I laughed. "Something like that." I lowered my voice. "I went for a walk with Caspian yesterday. My mother insisted," I added when his face dropped. "Anyway, the dragons came down the mountain yesterday. They surrounded Caspian and me."

Milo's eyes widened. "Woah, Azia! Thank the gods that you are all right. How did you escape? Did Caspian help you?"

I could see in his eyes that he didn't want to hear that Caspian had saved me. Luckily for him, he didn't have to.

"I saved us."

Before I could elaborate, the sound of my mother's voice came drifting through the door.

"Azia?"

Pushing Milo to one side quickly, I opened the door a crack.

"Sorry, Mother," I said, feigning a yawn. "I only just woke up."

"Azia, you know I deplore tardiness and breakfast has been laid out for ten minutes."

"I'm on my way," I singsonged, eager for her to leave should she see Milo behind me.

She held a hand to her mouth to cover a yawn, then turned and left, and I closed the door again.

"Sorry," I whispered, turning back to Milo. "I'll tell you after breakfast." I gave him a quick kiss then sprinted down the corridor after my mother.

In the dining hall, only my brothers were eating. "Where is Mother?" I asked Ash. "She only just came to get me."

Ash swallowed his cereal before addressing me. "Mother said she was tired and headed back to bed. Father is busy, and your boyfriend is with him. Something to do with dragons." He went back to his breakfast.

I assumed by boyfriend he was referring to the fae. I guess he told father about the dragons. I was surprised my mother hadn't knocked my bedroom door down to check if I was all right. I suspected that no one had told her. My father never kept secrets from her, but she'd been looking so ill recently that he probably didn't want to burden her.

At least, it solved the problem of having to tell my father about the dragons. Caspian was good for something, after all. When breakfast was over, I ran back upstairs.

"I'm glad you're here," Milo said when he saw me. He pulled me away from Jack and spoke again. "I've just been called to go outside. Your father knows about the dragons and wants most of the guards on outdoor duty today. I volunteered to check out the woods. I thought you might want to join me."

He looked at me so earnestly that I didn't have the heart to say no. Not that I wanted to say no.

I headed out first as not to arouse suspicion. With my mother asleep and my father out with the fae, it was unlikely anyone would see me slip out of the castle, but if they did, I would tell them I was going for a walk. I slipped out of the castle grounds by way of the door in the outer wall. I waited in the area we'd practiced fighting for Milo to arrive. Ten minutes later, and he was there, my sword in his hand.

"I hope you don't mind. I went into your room and picked up this. I thought you might like to practice what with there being dragons around. I still don't know how you survived them, but I'm pretty sure we are safe in here. The trees are too thick for dragons to get through."

He sat next to me on the rock. "So how did you escape the dragons?"

"I know magic," I explained, "I didn't know that I knew it, but Caspian showed me."

Milo's reaction was not what I expected. He stomped his foot down and turned away from me, his fists balled. "I don't trust that man."

I smiled at the ferociousness of his reaction. He'd barely ever seen the guy, and I'd talked so very little about him. This was jealousy. He was jealous because I was going to marry the fae. The smile faded from my lips. I was still going to marry Caspian. After what he told my mother, I would have no choice in the matter. My mother hadn't wanted me to be with Milo from the start, and now that she thought what we had was fake, she would never allow me to marry Milo instead. Not that I was ready to marry him either, but I'd rather share my days with the boy who kissed me first than that duplicitous creep.

"Let's fight," I said, picking up my sword and standing up. I turned him around to face me and kissed him lightly. Immediately his posture relaxed.

"We can't fight the way we did before. I couldn't carry out the armor we need. Today I'll teach you how to block, but we'll work slowly. That way, neither of us will get hurt."

We worked for hours, concentrating on posture before moving on to blocking. With each stroke of my sword, he showed me the correct way to block, first slowly and then when we'd both grown more confident in my ability, we speeded up. I wasn't set on hurting him, so none of my swipes were aimed at him, yet he danced around me, blocking each parry.

As my confidence increased, I began to copy him, until we were practically dancing around each other, the clank of our swords the only giveaway that this was no dance. Our swords were a blur as he threw in some attacks of his own. If we carried on this way, we would have no doubt slipped up and hurt each other, but a sneaky bit of tree root had me stumbling backward. Milo ran forward and caught my wrist. My sword fell to the ground, but I remained standing. He pulled me close until our faces were mere inches apart.

"You won," I whispered, my heart thumping in my chest. "What can I give you as the prize?"

He didn't answer, at least, not with words. He leaned forward and crushed his lips upon mine. All around us, snow began to fall again, but nothing mattered. Nothing at all but the here and now of the kiss with Milo and the realization that despite everything, I was falling in love with him.

Milo took my sword for me when it was time to go. We'd spent the whole morning practicing and then quite a bit of it kissing. I'd almost certainly missed lunch, and I was in danger of missing dinner too. I was surprised that my mother hadn't come looking for me. Perhaps she had but hadn't thought to check the woods. Why would she?

I left Milo and headed back into the castle, simultaneously feeling as light as a feather and broken-hearted at what I'd done and how my future was shaping up.

My heart had never felt so utterly bereft as it did now. How many times had I told myself over the past week that I didn't want or need a boyfriend? Falling for Milo had not been in the script at all, but now that our chances of dating were truly over, it made me want him all the more. Why hadn't I seen it from the start? Why hadn't I seen him? He'd been guarding my room every night for seven months, and it was only at the beginning of the year I'd really noticed him. If I'd thought to look up once in a while, I might have noticed him before. We could have been dating for months, and then, none of this would have happened. After months of dating, my mother would never try to force me to marry another man. Why had I been so stupid to let Caspian know that dating Milo had been fake?

My skin still tingled from where Milo had run his hand up my arm, my lips still felt the caress of his against them.

"Aza!" Remy shouted over at me as I stepped into the castle. He was sitting at the bottom of the main stairway, books surrounding him. When he saw I was looking at him, he waved his huge hand and beckoned me over. "Aza boo."

"Yes, I can see your books, Remy," I said only mildly impatiently. "You've been told about this before. Books belong in the library. You should only take one at a time." I moved forward and began to collect the books, but he grabbed my wrist.

"Aza, boo,"

"I'm picking them up. We have to take them back. Will you help?"

"No, Aza! Boo!" he strengthened the grip on my wrist and began to pull me upstairs.

"Remy stop. We've not picked up the books yet." I tried to pull against him, but he was too strong.

"Remy, let go!"

He shook his head and squeezed. Pain shot up my arm from where he squeezed me too tight. "Unsquash, Remy. Unsquash!"

He lessened his grip but didn't let go entirely.

"Is something wrong, Remy?" I asked, finally pulling my wrist from his hand. Giving it a rub to bring back the circulation, I looked into his eyes. I saw excitement in them. "Do you want to show me something?"

He danced up and down on the step, nodding his head. "Aza, boo."

"Ok, Remy, let's go." Sighing, I followed him up the stairs. He led me to the library.

The door to the precious books cabinet was open. It was the one part of the library that Remy was not allowed to touch, and he knew that. It was filled with books about the history of the Draconis Royal Family. Fear filled me as I realized the implications of this. Checking the books, I saw a space. One was missing.

"Remy," I said calmly. There was no point shouting at him. It would only freak him out, and I'd get nowhere. A quick scan of the library told me that the book was nowhere in sight. I thought back to the books at the bottom of the stairs. Most of them had been left open. I wondered if one of those had been the missing book, it couldn't have been. The old books were bound in leather. The ones downstairs had all been paper. "Where is the book?"

"Boo," he repeated and took my hand. This time I let him. He led me over to a table at the other side of the library. Under it, was the missing book. Ducking under the table, I reached out for it, breathing a sigh of relief to find it still in one piece.

"Aza!" Remy jabbed a finger at the page the book was open on.

"Is this what you wanted me to see?" I asked him. He clapped his hands together and danced on his feet, a beautiful grin, splitting his face.

Looking at the title, I saw it was one of the older history books of Draconis. I'd never read it before because it was horribly outdated. The section Remy wanted me to look at was about royal laws.

At first, nothing jumped out at me, but then something caught my eye.

Regarding marriages of the first daughter of the king and queen, if she is the eldest sibling, and therefore, the heir to the throne, she must be found a partner to marry if she cannot find one herself. If there are two or more suitors, the law states that a competition must be held to determine the man who the princess will marry. Any man in the land may enter, but usually, it is only the two men in question. These competitions were rare as most of the young princesses found a man themselves, but in one particularly strange incident over three hundred years ago when the monarchy was still young, Princess Bethel chose two men, both of whom died in the usually brutal competition. She ended up marrying a complete stranger. It didn't do her any harm. She went on to have sixteen children with him. For more details on the competition, turn to page seventy-three.

I didn't need to turn to page seventy-three. This was my way out of marrying Caspian that didn't involve going to prison for murder! I pulled Remy's face towards mine and gave him a kiss on the forehead. I was finally free of the madness, and there was nothing my mother or father could do about it. It was the law, no matter how outdated and sexist, and not even they were above it. Changing laws in the twelve kingdoms was a tricky endeavor and could sometimes take years. The king had to put the law forward, and the lawmakers of Urbis decided to pass it or not. I doubted my parents would want to wait years for me to marry Caspian, so they'd be forced into upholding the law. "Remy! You are a genius!"

Remy did another dance on the floor, and this time, I danced along with him. I was free of Caspian.

A noise shifted my attention away from our little soiree. I placed the royal history book back in the cabinet and went to investigate.

Outside the library and all over, the castle buzzed with people. Servants and guards ran this way and that in a state of what I could only describe as panic.

If they were all running in one direction, I could understand it, but there seemed to be no rhyme or reason to the chaos.

Fear gripped me as I thought about the dragons. Had they come back? Were we being attacked?

"What's happening?" I asked a maid who was passing by, with what looked to be a wet cloth in her hands.

"I can't tell you." She burst into tears and ran off towards the main staircase.

Following the maid to the second floor, the chaos was even more pronounced here. A gaggle of people stood outside my parents' room. Most of them worked at the castle. Some, I didn't recognize at all. They all spoke over each other, so it was impossible to tell what any of them were saying. The maid with the cloth practically screeched, making everyone move back. As the crowd moved, those at the back noticed me. A whisper went among them, and suddenly, they were all quiet and looking at me, pity filling their eyes.

"What is it?" I whispered, not daring to move. The path the maid had made between them widened to allow me to pass through.

With each step I took toward them, my heart rate increased, and as I passed, they all lowered their heads. Inside the room, my mother lay on the bed, her face ashen, her eyes closed. Beside her, my father held her hand as the maid mopped my mother's brow and someone I didn't know checked her pulse.

"Father..." I started, walking toward the bed.

When he looked over in my direction, a stab of fear

clutched at my heart. He had tears in his eyes. I'd never seen my father cry. Not once in my whole life.

"She's alive," he said, holding out his other hand to me.

I glanced back toward my mother again. She looked like the mother I knew well. Gone were the dark circles under her eyes and the blotchy skin. She looked perfect in every way. Underneath the thin sheet covering her, I saw the rhythmical rise and fall of her chest as she breathed. Her eyes remained shut.

"What happened?"

"I don't know," my father said quietly. "She's not been feeling well for days. She came for a nap this morning, and when her personal maid came to wake her, she wouldn't wake up."

At this, the maid with the cloth burst into tears.

"I'm sorry, Your Majesty. Forgive me." She ran from the room, taking the cloth with her. I followed her with my line of sight to find the people still looking in. In my father's worry, he'd allowed the staff to congregate. I let go of my father's hand and marched to the door.

"Please leave us. We will let you know what is happening as soon as we ascertain the situation ourselves. Please carry on as normal. I'll meet you all in the grand hall at seven o'clock and fill you all in. Please pass the word to the other members of the staff and don't let word of this get out to the public." I closed the door. That speech was my very first act as a leader. My father was in no fit state to be a king today. He deserved a day off after eighteen years of service without one. I would take that meeting, and I would tell everyone what was happening. I'd tell my brothers too. Once I knew what it was that was happening myself.

"Do you know what is wrong with her, doctor?" I'd not been introduced to him, but it didn't take a genius to figure out who he was.

"Her vital signs are normal. Her breathing is normal, her heart rate is normal. It would appear that she is just asleep, Your Highness."

A thrill of fear passed through me. My father's face drained of the little color it already had. I'm sure that to literally anyone else, the fact that she was perfectly healthy would be a comfort, but my mother had been in this situation before, and that time, she'd not awoken for a hundred years.

"I've never seen anything like this before," the doctor continued. "I see no reason why she won't wake up. If you let me take her to Zhore, I could have my partners run tests on her."

"She's not leaving this room," my father uttered, his jaw clenched. "Get your partners in here if you must, but she stays."

The doctor nodded, taking his stethoscope and putting it in his bag.

"I'm not sure it will help. I don't want to be the one to say this, but I think this is a little out of my realm. I don't think this is an illness. I think this is a curse."

The anguished cries of my father rang through the castle. After eighteen years, my mother was Sleeping Beauty once more.

Continue the adventure in Heiress of Embers

A NOTE FROM THE AUTHOR

The Kingdom of Fairytales authors hope you enjoyed this new way of reading. We don't think that a series has ever been set with one chapter a day thought a whole year before and we hope we did it justice.

With this in mind, please leave a review, but when you do, remember that these books were always meant to be short breaks in your day and the blurb reflects that.

We would LOVE it if you can drop us a few words on Amazon

Review here

AFTER THE HAPPILY EVER AFTER...

There is more to these stories. You want to know what happens next right? Fast forward eighteen years...

Pick up book one now

PREQUEL

SLEEPING BEAUTY

1. Queen of Dragons
2. Heiress of Embers
3. Throne of Fury
4. Goddess of Flames

LITTLE MERMAID

5. Queen of Mermaids
6. Heiress of the Sea
7. Throne of Change
8. Goddess of Water

RED RIDING HOOD

9. King of Wolves

10. Heir of the Curse
11. Throne of Night
12. God of Shifters

RAPUNZEL

13. King of Devotion
14. Heir of Thorns
15. Throne of Enchantment
16. God of Loyalty

RUMPELSTILTSKIN

17. Queen of Unicorns
18. Heiress of Gold
19. Throne of Sacrifice
20. Goddess of Loss

BEAUTY AND THE BEAST

21. King of Beasts
22. Heir of Beauty
23. Throne of Betrayal
24. God of Illusion

ALADDIN

25. Queen of the Sun
26. Heiress of Shadows
27. Throne of the Phoenix
28. Goddess of Fire

CINDERELLA

29. Queen of Song
30. Heiress of Melody
31. Throne of Symphony
32. Goddess of Harmony

ALICE IN WONDERLAND

33. Queen of Clockwork
34. Heiress of Delusion
35. Throne of Cards
36. Goddess of Hearts

WIZARD OF OZ

37. King of Traitors
38. Heir of Fugitives
39. Throne of Emeralds
40. God of Storms

SNOW WHITE

41. Queen of Reflections
42. Heiress of Mirrors
43. Throne of Wands
44. Goddess of Magic

PETER PAN

45. Queen of Skies
46. Heiress of Stars
47. Throne of Feathers
48. Goddess of Air

URBIS

49. Kingdom of Royalty
50. Kingdom of Power
51. Kingdom of Fairytales
52. Kingdom of Ever After

JOIN US

Would you like a FREE Kingdom of Fairytales gift? Click the link below to pick your free gift up.

Kingdom of Fairytales FREE gift

Check the Kingdom of Fairytales website for competitions, news and info on all the books and authors

Kingdom of Fairytales Website

Or Join us on our Kingdom of Fairytales Facebook page for fun, games and author takeovers

Still want more? Completely immerse yourself in the Kingdom of Fairytales experience and pick up exclusive offers and gifts

Become a Patron

THE KINGDOM OF FAIRYTALES TEAM

These books would not be written without a great many people. Here is our team:

Many thanks to those who have made this possible.

Thank you to Rhi Parkes without whom, this series would never have come about.

Thanks to all the authors.

J.A. Armitage, Audrey Rich, B. Kristen Mcmichael, Emma Savant, Jennifer Ellision, Scarlett Kol, R. Castro, Margo Ryerkerk, Zara Quentin, Laura Greenwood and Anne Stryker

Also thank you to our amazing Beta team

Nadine Peterse-Vrijhof, Diane Major, Kalli Bunch and Stephanie Pittser.

Thanks to our Proof Reader

Tina Merritt

ABOUT THE AUTHOR

J.A lives in a total fantasy world (because reality is boring right?) When she's not writing all the crazy fun in her head, she can be found eating cake, designing pretty pictures and hanging upside down from the tallest climbing frame in the local playground while her children look on in embarrassment. She's travelled the world working as everything from a banana picker in Australia to a Pantomime clown, has climbed to the top of Mount Kilimanjaro and the bottom of the Grand Canyon and once gave birth to a surrogate baby for a friend of hers.

She spends way too much time gossiping on facebook and if you want to be part of her Reading Army, where you'll get lots of freebies, exclusive sneak peeks and super secret sales, join up here

https://www.subscribepage.com/v7o8k4

Somehow she finds time to write.

Printed in Great Britain
by Amazon

60696964R00083